THE DOCKLAND MURDER

An Augusta Peel Mystery Book 9

EMILY ORGAN

The Augusta Peel Series

Death in Soho
Murder in the Air
The Bloomsbury Murder
The Tower Bridge Murder
Death in Westminster
Murder on the Thames
The Baker Street Murders
Death in Kensington
The Dockland Murder

Chapter 1

Dawn glowed in the east as Police Constable Buller paced along the quayside of West India Dock. The sweep of his torch beam on the cobblestones sent rats scuttling into the dark shadows of the warehouses. Ship masts, funnels and cranes were silhouetted against the ash grey sky. The sweet, smoky scent of rum from the warehouses mingled with the smell of brine, oil and tar.

Beyond the warehouses came the distant sound of an early morning train rumbling into the goods station. Constable Buller's stomach gave a grumble, it was almost five o'clock but another two hours until his breakfast time.

He shone his torch at the hull of each ship as he passed it. The *Meerdrecht* from Antwerp, *Appomattox* from Philadelphia, and *Juno* from Naples. These ships were moored in the import dock so their cargo could be unloaded by East London's dockworkers. While in port, the sailors from the ships were enjoying their shore leave in the public houses and cheap hotels of Limehouse and Poplar.

As he approached the *Colonia*, a London registered

ship, Constable Buller's torchlight fell upon a bundle of clothing. But then he saw feet and something pale. A face.

A man lay on the ground. Constable Buller ran up to him.

'Hello?' There was no response.

The man lay on his side, his eyes open and staring. Only now could the constable see the injuries to the back of the man's head. The blood was a stark, shiny red in the torch's beam.

A top hat lay close by on the cobbles. The man was smartly dressed in a dark woollen overcoat. He wore black leather gloves and his shoes were polished to shine.

The constable blew his whistle for help.

Constable Milton arrived moments later. 'Good grief!' he said. 'That's not who I think it is, is it?'

'Yes,' said Constable Buller. 'I'm afraid it is.'

Both constables knew the gentleman they were looking at. His waxed grey moustache, sharp features and pale blue eyes were unmistakable.

Chapter 2

'IT'S NO USE,' SAID AUGUSTA. 'I HAVE TO PUT THIS DOWN!'

Her arms strained with pain as she staggered towards the nearest bench in Russell Square. She dropped the box onto it and rubbed her upper arms. 'Hopeless,' she said. 'I thought I had more strength than that!'

'Let me carry it the rest of the way,' said Fred as he rested his box next to Augusta's.

'It's fine, I'll manage. You've got your own box to carry.'

'I can come back for it. Don't you want to put your box down, Harriet?'

'Oh, alright then.'

The strength of the young woman astonished Augusta. She was a slender, slight young thing and yet a heavy box of books was no trouble for her at all.

A cool breeze whirled around the square, carrying a few early autumn leaves with it. A squirrel scampered across the lawn to a large oak, then scurried up its trunk. Augusta surveyed the three boxes of books on the bench and thought about the time needed to repair them all.

'Do you think you would like to learn how to repair books?' she asked Fred.

'Me? I'd love to!' He grinned.

'Good. I shall teach you then. It's going to take me months to repair all these on my own.'

'It's a very kind donation from the family of the late Edith Chambers, isn't it?' said Fred.

'Yes, very kind indeed. I certainly don't want to appear ungrateful. I just wish we'd found a car or van to take them in.'

'We don't have much further to go now,' said Fred. 'If you want to wait here with your box, I'll come back for it.'

'No, it's alright.' Augusta circled her arms, preparing to pick up the box again. 'I've already got this far, I can manage the last few hundred yards.'

'Are you sure?'

'Absolutely.'

Secretly, Augusta didn't wish to be outdone by Harriet. She rubbed her palms together, took in a breath, and lifted the box.

It felt even heavier than before.

'Let's go!' she said, staggering off across the square.

Someone was waiting for them outside the shop. A stout, grey-haired gentleman in a dark suit and overcoat.

'Detective Inspector Morris?' said Augusta. She'd worked with the Scotland Yard detective previously. She lowered the box of books to the ground, gasping as soon as she'd released the weight.

'Hello, Mrs Peel. Your shop is closed, I see.'

'Yes, we had to collect some books from a lady in Cartwright Gardens.'

'You've carried that box all the way from there?'

'Yes.' Augusta shook her arms. They were weak and trembling from the effort.

'I'll unlock the shop,' said Fred.

'I buzzed Mr Fisher's bell as well,' said Morris. 'But there was no reply. Is he still away seeing his family in Worthing?'

'Yes he is,' said Augusta. Philip had been away for ten days. Augusta hoped he wasn't getting on too well with his estranged wife. Then she felt unkind for thinking it.

Fred opened the shop door and Morris picked up Augusta's box of books and carried it in. 'Where do you want this?' he asked.

'Just follow Fred and Harriet to the workshop at the back,' she said. 'Thank you, Detective.'

Her arms felt barely strong enough to pick up the bag of birdseed from behind the counter and feed some to Sparky the canary. His cage sat on the countertop.

'Shall I make some tea?' said Harriet, emerging from the workshop.

'Thank you.' Augusta smiled. Fred and Harriet had been courting for a few weeks and Harriet had become a regular visitor to the shop. She was helpful and also good at making tea.

'Will you stay for tea, Detective Inspector Morris?' Augusta asked. She wasn't yet sure why he was here.

'That would be lovely, thank you, Mrs Peel.' He wandered over to the bookshelves and took out a book. 'This looks interesting. *British Sport Past And Present* by E D Cuming.' He leafed through its pages.

'Was there anything in particular you wished to see Mr Fisher about?' asked Augusta.

'Oh yes, I almost forgot myself. It's easy to get distracted in a shop like this.' He replaced the book. 'I didn't come here to speak to Fisher. It's you who I wish to speak to, Mrs Peel.'

'Me?'

'Yes.' He strolled back to the counter and made a little clucking noise at Sparky. 'You've heard all about the unpleasant business in the dockyard two days ago?'

'The murder of Sir Graywood?'

'That's right. It's very puzzling indeed. I thought I would come and speak to you about it, given your personal connection to the case.'

'Personal connection?' said Augusta. 'I don't understand.'

'Oh. Didn't you know? Sir Frederick Graywood was your uncle, Mrs Peel.'

Chapter 3

AUGUSTA SUGGESTED TO DETECTIVE INSPECTOR MORRIS
that they continue their conversation in her workshop.
They sat on stools at her workbench with their cups of tea
which Harriet had made.

'Sir Graywood married your aunt fifteen years ago,'
said Morris.

'Which aunt?'

'Your Aunt Lydia, I believe. Your father's sister.'

The mention of her father made her shoulders tense.
'I've had nothing to do with my family for twenty years.'

'So I understand. I recall Fisher mentioning something
along those lines to me. So you never met Sir Graywood?'

'No. I know nothing about him. The last time I saw my
Aunt Lydia was twenty-five years ago at my cousin's
wedding. She and my father weren't close.'

Augusta recalled her cousin Violet's wedding at a pretty
church in Northumberland. She'd been fifteen at the time.
Aunt Lydia had worn an enormous hat covered with bright
spring flowers and had stolen much of the attention from
her daughter. In those days, Aunt Lydia had been married

to Uncle Noel and they'd had five children. Augusta wondered what had happened to Uncle Noel. And how had her aunt ended up marrying the shipping magnate, Sir Frederick Graywood?

'I wish to offer you my condolences on the death of your uncle, Mrs Peel,' said Detective Inspector Morris.

'Thank you. Although I never knew him, so I can't say I'm suffering personally from his loss. The murder of anyone, however, is tragic. I read about his death in the newspaper. What are the details?'

'Sir Graywood's body was found by a constable from the Port of London Authority police. He was on night patrol on the northern West India Dock and found Sir Graywood lying on the quayside shortly before five o'clock in the morning. He appears to have been attacked with a heavy object, although no murder weapon has been found yet. There's a good possibility it was thrown into the water which means we have very little chance of recovering it. I don't know if you've ever visited the dockyards, Mrs Peel, but those docks are enormous.'

'Was it usual for Sir Graywood to be on the quayside at night?'

'No. Very unusual.'

'Did he tell anyone he was going there?'

'No, he appears to have kept his plans to himself. He was found close to one of his ships, the *Colonia*. It had arrived the previous day from Antwerp. The doctor who examined Sir Graywood says he died from several blows to the head. There were injuries to his hands and arms too which suggests he tried to defend himself.'

'Do you know what time he was attacked?'

'The constable on patrol that night says he passed through that section of the dock at half-past two and saw nothing untoward. Then, at three o'clock, he heard a noise from one of the warehouses. Apparently, it sounded like someone had got in. So he whistled for his colleague who was patrolling the southern West India dock, and the pair spent a good hour searching for the source of the noise. They found nothing and no sign of a break-in. So they resumed their patrols, and he found Sir Graywood's body shortly before five. The doctor thinks Sir Graywood died sometime between three and half-past four.'

'It sounds like the murderer made a noise to distract the constables,' said Augusta.

'Yes, it's possible. This attack was clearly well-planned.'

'There could have been more than one of them. One to distract the night watchman and the other to attack Sir Graywood.'

'That's certainly a possibility, too.'

'When was Sir Graywood last seen before his murder?'

'He dined at his club on Pall Mall and left about midnight.'

'And he went to the dockyard from there?'

'It seems so. He didn't return to his home in Mayfair.'

'Did he tell anyone in the club he was going to the dockyard?'

'No.'

'Do you know how he got there?'

'He asked the doorman at the club to hail a cab for him. We're looking for the cab driver who drove him there. It's a journey of about six miles and could have taken fifteen or twenty minutes at that time of night. About half the time it would take in the day.'

'So he didn't tell anyone he was going there,' said Augusta. 'But he must have told someone because his attacker knew he would be there. The attacker also knew they had to distract the constables on night patrol before they attacked him.'

'Good point.'

'So what was he doing there? And did he arrange to meet someone?'

'Very important questions, Mrs Peel. He was found lying close to one of the ships he owned. That suggests to me he planned to go on board the *Colonia*, possibly with the purpose of examining or unloading some of its cargo.'

'By himself?'

'He couldn't have unloaded any of the cargo by himself. And we don't know yet if anything was unloaded that night. But the fact he was there at that hour suggests something clandestine to me.'

'Illegal?'

'It pains me to say it because he was your uncle, Mrs Peel.'

'He was the husband of my aunt who I haven't seen for twenty-five years. I never knew him, and I'm willing to consider he could have been doing something illegal.'

'But everyone I've spoken to so far refuses to believe it of the man. He was extremely successful and held in high regard by everyone who knew him. His second in command, a chap called Captain Pegwell, is devastated by this incident. He swears blind that Sir Graywood wasn't up to anything illicit that night.'

'But that doesn't mean he wasn't.'

'No.' The detective took a sip of tea and sighed. 'There's a lot to learn about this case yet. I'm wondering if you would like to accompany me to visit your aunt, Lady Graywood.'

Augusta's heart gave a heavy thud. 'My aunt? But I don't really know her.'

'I've spoken to her briefly, and she's extremely distressed,' said Morris. 'I need to visit her again and I think your presence will help put her at ease.'

'Or make her feel even worse!' said Augusta with a laugh. 'How did you find out she was my aunt? I've kept my family details extremely private.'

'I'm a detective,' said Morris. 'I can find these things out.'

Augusta sipped her tea as she thought. She didn't like the idea of speaking to anyone in her family again. 'Aunt Lydia won't be happy to see me,' she said. 'I feel sure of it. My parents tried to force me to marry a man I didn't love. They arranged the wedding without my knowledge, so I had to leave. That's when I came to London.'

'Was your aunt involved in any of it?'

'No.'

'So even though you're estranged from your parents, Mrs Peel, you're not actually estranged from your aunt?'

'No. But she's probably heard disparaging things about me.'

'From your parents?'

'Yes. Especially my father. He's her brother. I'm sure her mind will be set against me.'

'Do you know that for sure?'

'No, I don't.'

The detective drained his cup. 'That's probably one of the best cups of tea I've had in a long time.'

'Harriet made it. She's very good at it.'

'She certainly is. Perhaps it's best if I leave you to think about your involvement in this case, Mrs Peel? I think you would be extremely helpful, but I also understand that it could be difficult for you to speak to someone in your family again.'

'Thank you, Detective Inspector Morris. I'll certainly give it some thought.'

They got off their stools and headed for the door.

Augusta thought of Sir Graywood the shipping

magnate and what could have led him to visit one of his ships in the middle of the night. And who had been lying in wait for him there?

In the shop, Morris took *British Sport Past And Present* off the shelf. 'I think I shall buy this,' he said. 'It's my sort of book.'

Fred served the detective while Augusta continued to think about Sir Graywood. How had Aunt Lydia come to marry him? What had happened to her first husband, Uncle Noel?

If she refused to help Morris, then she might never find out the answers to her questions.

'I've thought about it,' she said as Fred handed the detective his book in a brown paper bag. 'I'd like to help.'

'Are you sure, Mrs Peel?'

'Absolutely sure.'

'You don't want more time to think about it?'

'No. I want to help.'

Morris smiled. 'Thank you. I'd like to visit your aunt tomorrow, if that's alright. How about we meet in Mayfair at ten? At the corner of Grosvenor Square and Upper Grosvenor Street.'

Augusta smiled. 'I shall see you then, Detective.'

Chapter 4

HALF AN HOUR AFTER DETECTIVE INSPECTOR MORRIS HAD left the shop, the door was flung open and Lady Hereford was pushed inside in her bath chair.

'Augusta, Augusta!'

'Oh dear, what's happened?'

'There's something I need to tell you.' The nurse hurriedly wheeled Lady Hereford up to the counter. 'Have you heard about the murder of Sir Graywood in the West India docks?' Her eyes twinkled excitedly and her face was flushed beneath the pink circles of rouge.

'Yes, I—'

'Let me finish a moment. Do you realise who he was? I've just discovered it today. He was your uncle, Augusta!'

'Yes. I know.'

Lady Hereford's face fell. 'You know?'

'Yes. A detective from Scotland Yard told me.'

'How did he know?'

'I don't know.'

'He's clearly a good detective then.'

'He's asked me to help him with the case. He thinks I

can help him speak to Lady Graywood who's my father's sister, Aunt Lydia.'

'Yes! That's what I wanted to tell you. But you already knew it, so there was no need for me to rush here. I should have just telephoned. And that would have been a waste of time too because you already knew.' Lady Hereford sighed. 'How's my little Sparky?'

The canary cocked his head and surveyed her from his perch in his cage.

'He's very well,' said Augusta. 'He has quite an appetite on him at the moment.'

'Don't give into him.' Lady Hereford wagged a cautionary finger at her. 'He's very good at begging.'

The canary fluttered his wings.

'I know what you're trying to do, Sparky,' said Lady Hereford. 'You're trying to charm me and it's working very well indeed.' She gave Augusta a smile and Augusta handed her the bag of birdseed.

'So you're going to help with the investigation into your uncle's death,' said the old lady as she fed Sparky some seed.

'Yes. Although it's odd hearing him referred to in that way as I didn't know him.'

'Yes, I suppose it must be rather strange. And it will be interesting for you to meet your Aunt Lydia after all these years.'

'Did you ever know her well?' Augusta asked. Lady Hereford had been a good friend of Augusta's family, but she had sided with Augusta when she'd left them.

'Not very well. She was a terrible snob. Even worse than your father. I haven't seen her for many years.'

'Do you know anything about Sir Graywood?'

'Not a great deal. He came from a fairly ordinary family, as I recall. His father and uncle set up a shipping company in Newcastle or Glasgow, or somewhere up north. Then he took it over and made such an enormous success of it that he was made a viscount by the prime minister in those days, Mr Balfour. He was widowed and had a son at the time of his engagement to your aunt. Lydia invited me to their wedding but I'm ashamed to say I didn't attend.'

'Why are you ashamed?'

'Well, it's rude to turn down a wedding invitation, isn't it? But I never had much time for Lydia. And I imagined I'd be sat at a table at that wedding with lots of shipping people and I wouldn't know the first thing to say to them. I know nothing about shipping. Or the sea, for that matter. I get terribly seasick. I used to dread it whenever Lord Hereford and I visited America. Those crossings were insufferable. The Atlantic is such an unpredictable ocean.'

'I hadn't realised Aunt Lydia had remarried,' said Augusta. 'I remember when she was married to Uncle Noel and I went to cousin Violet's wedding.'

'That was a dreadful wedding,' said Lady Hereford. 'They got married in a draughty church in Northumberland somewhere. And that enormous house they lived in was draughtier still. It was the middle of July and I was as cold as a block of ice the entire day.'

'Yes, I remember that.'

'You would have been very young at the time, Augusta. You were only about three.'

'I was fifteen.'

'Fifteen? Goodness. Are you really that old these days?'

'I'm afraid so. Do you know what happened to Uncle Noel?'

'Yes, he drowned in the Lake District. Fell off a boat and that was that. I heard he was a drinker, so it wouldn't surprise me if he'd been under the influence of alcohol at the time. Anyway, this death of Sir Graywood is certainly a puzzle. What was he doing at the dockyard at that unearthly hour?'

'It seems he was checking on his ship.'

'In the middle of the night? There has to be something suspicious about that.'

'Detective Inspector Morris hasn't found anyone yet who knows why he was there.'

'Very mysterious. What does Mr Fisher make of it?'

'I haven't discussed it with him yet,' said Augusta. 'He's still on the south coast, visiting his family.'

'His wife?'

'Yes, and his son. He was worried about them after threats were made against them while we were investigating the Kensington murder case.'

'That must have been extremely unpleasant for him. How long is he spending on the south coast?'

'I don't know. But he's been there for ten days so far.'

'Ten days?' Lady Hereford raised an eyebrow. 'That's quite a long time. Perhaps he and his wife plan to reconcile.'

'Perhaps.' The thought left an unpleasant taste in Augusta's mouth. 'But I don't see why he would want to reconcile after she had a love affair with his friend.'

'Some people can be very forgiving. Especially when they love someone.'

Augusta wished Lady Hereford would change the topic of conversation.

'There's a young son too,' continued the old lady. 'That's another good reason to mend the marriage.'

'Yes, I suppose it is.'

Augusta knew it was important for Philip to be reunited with his family again. But the thought made her envious, and then she felt guilty about her jealousy. An opportunity to have a relationship with Philip had arisen during their time working together during the war. But she'd been too grief stricken back then to consider it. Her fiancé at the time, Matthew Peel, had been killed at the Battle of Loos.

'Oh dear, Augusta,' said Lady Hereford. 'You look quite unhappy. Is everything alright?'

Augusta forced a smile. 'Yes. Everything's fine. I suppose I'm nervous about meeting Aunt Lydia tomorrow.'

'I wouldn't worry too much about her.'

'But she might tell my father all about our meeting.'

'She might. But she may not take a great deal of interest in you, Augusta. I'm afraid the person she cares about the most is herself.'

Chapter 5

STATELY GEORGIAN BUILDINGS FORMED THE SIDES OF Grosvenor Square. In the centre sat a pleasant rectangle of green with immaculate lawns and mature trees.

Augusta waited on the corner at the junction of Upper Grosvenor Street. A well-dressed lady walked past with a tiny dog on a long lead. Detective Inspector Morris arrived after ten minutes.

'Sorry I'm late,' he puffed. 'Lots of hold ups on the Central London tube. Now then, are you sure you're happy to meet with your estranged aunt, Mrs Peel?'

'Absolutely sure.'

'Good. Well, hopefully Lady Graywood will feel like talking to us today.'

They made their way through the refined streets of Mayfair. Aunt Lydia's home had a grand black door with a gleaming brass knocker and a brass number five.

A shiny blue Napier limousine was parked outside the house and a chauffeur was polishing it with a rag. He greeted them with a nod.

A maid admitted them to an entrance hall with a

polished black-and-white floor and a high ceiling with a glittering chandelier.

They waited while the maid took Morris's card to her employer. She returned a few moments later. 'Lady Graywood has requested that your meeting with her be quick,' she said. 'She's feeling very tired today.'

'Of course.' Morris removed his hat. 'We don't intend to detain Lady Graywood any longer than is necessary.'

Augusta felt her heart thud as they followed the maid to the drawing room. What was Aunt Lydia's reaction to her going to be? Would she be angry? Upset? Happy?

The drawing room was deep burgundy and gold, with plush armchairs and a long, comfortable sofa. Above the marble fireplace hung a large painting of a ship at sea, battling against fierce waves. Glass cabinets housed porcelain figurines and exotic artefacts. A lean black cat with narrow eyes watched them from a windowsill.

Aunt Lydia reclined on the sofa, dressed in black satin. Her sharp green eyes immediately reminded Augusta of her father. She caught her breath and managed to smile.

She estimated her aunt was in her mid-sixties now. Her features were classically refined, with high cheekbones and a short, pointed nose. Her auburn hair was faded to a distinguished grey.

'Lady Graywood.' Morris gave a reverent bow. 'Thank you for agreeing to see me again. This is Mrs Augusta Peel. I believe you've met before?'

Aunt Lydia stared at Augusta, then her brow furrowed. 'Rebecca?'

'So you do remember me, Aunt Lydia? I'm very sorry to hear about the death of your husband.'

'Where've you been all these years?'

'Here in London.'

'And you have a new name?'

'I called myself Augusta Peel during the war and the name has remained.'

'Mrs? So you're married?'

'No. I just use Mrs. It's easier that way.'

Aunt Lydia frowned. 'This is very confusing, I don't quite understand. Why are you here with the police?'

'Mrs Peel is a talented lady,' said Morris. 'She's assisted Scotland Yard with several cases over the past couple of years, so I've asked for her help today. While investigating this case, I discovered Mrs Peel was related to you.'

'She is indeed. Although I know her as Rebecca and I can't think why she works with the police.'

'I own a secondhand bookshop, too.'

'Do you? How peculiar.'

Augusta realised that Aunt Lydia considered a shop-keeper to be a low-class occupation.

'The purpose of my visit today is to ask you some more questions about your husband, Lady Graywood,' said the detective.

'How far have you got with it all?' she asked.

'Not terribly far just yet, my lady. That's why I've asked Mrs Peel to help.'

She gave a laugh. 'My niece! This really does feel very strange. You must have been a girl when I last saw you, Rebecca.'

'It was at Violet's wedding. I was fifteen.'

'Yes, that would be about right.'

'How is Violet?'

'She's well. Still married to the duke and they have four delightful children. Well, they're not children anymore, they're quite grown up. The youngest, Sophia, is eighteen now.'

'And I hear Uncle Noel died a few years ago. I was sorry to hear it.'

'Yes, that was sixteen years ago. This is the second time I've been widowed.' She gave a thin smile. 'I suppose some could accuse me of being careless.'

'I only discovered Sir Graywood was my uncle yesterday.'

'That's what happens when you remove yourself from your family. You miss out on these things. You'll never know him, Rebecca, and yet he was a wonderful man.' She pulled a black handkerchief from her sleeve and wiped her eyes with it.

The maid brought in tea and Augusta and Morris made themselves comfortable in the pair of velvet chairs next to the sofa.

Morris took out his notebook. 'We had a brief conversation two days ago, Lady Graywood, and you were understandably too distressed to tell me much. The purpose of my visit today is to find out as much as I can about your husband's movements leading up to his tragic death. Can you tell me when you last saw him?'

Chapter 6

AUNT LYDIA SIGHED. 'I'VE EXPLAINED ALL THIS TO A sergeant at the Port of London police.'

'I appreciate that, Lady Graywood,' said Morris. 'And I'm sorry you're having to explain things twice over. I'm from Scotland Yard, you see. We're separate from the Port of London police.'

'But can't you chaps at least talk to each other?'

'We do talk to each other, my lady. But it's also quite useful having two statements from you to compare.'

'Compare? Are you trying to find inconsistencies, Detective?'

'Not necessarily.' He scratched his temple, clearly concerned he was upsetting her. 'It's possible that while you're talking to me and Mrs Peel you'll remember something you forgot to mention to the Port of London police.'

'I think you do this to catch people out. After all, if I'm lying, then I might forget what lies I've come up with and tell you something different. That's how you trip people up, Detective. I'm not stupid.'

'Of course you're not, Lady Graywood. I don't believe you're lying, nor am I trying to catch you out. I would merely like to hear your account. I'm sure your niece would like to hear it too.'

Aunt Lydia gave Augusta a sharp look.

'Very well,' she said. 'But I want it known that this is all taking a terrible toll on my nerves. I have just been widowed in the most shocking of ways. I should be resting and not having to endure this.'

'I realise that, Lady—'

'No, I don't think you do, Detective. Otherwise you wouldn't be making me repeat myself.' She dabbed her eyes with her handkerchief. 'Right. I shall explain again what happened and I don't expect to have to repeat myself after this. You need to get out there and look for my husband's killer.'

'Of course, Lady Graywood.'

'I last saw Frederick at breakfast that morning. He had his usual boiled egg followed by kippers, then toast and marmalade. He drank his tea, read his post and read his newspaper. Frederick was always a man of few words in the mornings, so we didn't speak much. After his breakfast, he rolled up his newspaper, gave me a kiss on the cheek and told me he was having dinner at his club that evening and that he planned to spend the night there so not to disturb the household with his late return.'

'Was that common?' asked Morris.

'Yes, quite common.'

'And your husband didn't mention any plans to visit the dockyard that night?'

'No.'

'Do you think it's unusual he didn't tell you he was planning to go there?'

'No. Something must have come up. Perhaps he got a telephone call at the club late that evening summoning him there.'

'We don't have a record of that happening.'

'It doesn't mean it didn't though, did it? You chaps miss things all the time.'

'Who could have telephoned your husband at the club late that night, summoning him to the dockyard?'

'I don't know! That's the sort of thing you should be finding out. Pegwell might have called him, check with him.'

Augusta sipped her tea. She thought her aunt was being argumentative and irritable. She wondered if it was a usual character trait or a reaction to the shock of her husband's death.

'Had Sir Graywood ever been called out to the dock-yard at night before?'

'Once or twice, I believe. There was a break-in at one of the warehouses a few years ago, and Frederick had to get there in the middle of the night. There was once a fire on one of his ships, too. Not a serious one, but he had to attend to it. Perhaps some dockers were misbehaving, refusing to unload a cargo or something like that. Those people like to complain about their pay and working conditions. Quite ridiculous really, they should be grateful for the work!'

'But you have no idea why your husband went to the dock that night?'

'No. No idea at all. Had he been here when he received the telephone call, then he would have told me. But he was at the club.'

'Do you think it's possible he arranged to meet someone there?'

'No, I can't imagine that at all. Why would my husband arrange to meet someone in the middle of the night? I don't have the answers I'm afraid, Detective. All this happened while I was asleep.'

'Can you think of anyone your husband may have had a disagreement with? Someone in the company or a business rival?'

'I can't think of anyone. That doesn't mean to say there isn't someone he fell out with. He could be quite ruthless. He had to be to achieve his success. And many people envied him, of course.'

'Such as who?'

'Rival shipping men. I don't want to name names as they could all be entirely innocent. But look them up yourself, Detective. I've little doubt they envied the ships and the contracts he had. It's a competitive business and there's good money to be made. Why don't you find these men and ask them yourself? Frederick was proud of his company and enjoyed being the very best. It would have made many people jealous, and it's down to you, Detective, to find out who those people are. I simply don't know enough about it. I stayed out of it most of the time, to be honest with you. There really is nothing more boring than shipping.'

'So your theory is your husband was murdered by a business rival?'

'I can't think of any other possible reason. Now I've just told you everything I've told the sergeant from the dockyard police. I don't expect to repeat it again.' She drained her cup of tea.

'Sir Graywood leaves a son, am I right?'

'Yes.' Her lips thinned. 'Rupert.'

'I shall need to speak with him.'

'Please do. He's in apartment number five at Wentworth Mansions, just off Piccadilly. Now would you excuse me, Detective, while I take a turn with my niece in the garden? Her appearance here today has quite puzzled me and I have a few words I wish to say to her in private.'

Augusta's stomach gave an anxious flip.

Chapter 7

IN THE GARDEN, AUNT LYDIA TOOK AUGUSTA'S ARM AND led her along a path towards a summer house. Early autumn flowers bloomed in colours of yellow, dark pink and red. It was a small garden, bordered on all sides by a tall brick wall. But it was large enough for a spacious lawn with a fountain in the centre. Aunt Lydia's black satin dress rustled as she walked while a rabble of noisy starlings chattered in a nearby tree.

'I still find it difficult to believe it's really you, Rebecca. And spending your time with the police! It's very strange.'

'What's wrong with the police?' asked Augusta.

'There's nothing wrong with them as they are. They do an important job, even if they can be irritating at times by asking you to repeat things you've already told them. But it's the association…'

'Because my father is an earl?'

'Yes. I don't understand your need to associate with people of a lower class.'

'I associate with people of all classes, Aunt Lydia. I

don't consider anyone to be superior by the mere virtue of their birth.'

'Goodness.' Her lips pursed. 'You're one of those socialist types, are you?'

'No. But I think the class system in this country does a lot of damage.'

Aunt Lydia withdrew her arm. 'Your feelings clearly haven't changed since you left the family.'

'No, they haven't.'

Her aunt stopped and fixed her gaze. 'You were born into enormous privilege, Rebecca. It astonishes me that you chose to walk away from it.'

Augusta felt her teeth clench. 'I walked away because my family was forcing me to marry a man I didn't love. It wasn't choice, it was necessity.'

'It's often a requirement for ladies of our class, Rebecca. Do you think the generations of ladies before you married for love? Not often. They did it for duty. They respected the pedigree of their families and helped forge the necessary alliances. Our prestigious families are responsible for leading this great country and its empire. Without us, it would fail. Do you want Britain to go the way of Russia? Do you want the Bolsheviks in charge?'

'No. And there are no Bolsheviks in Britain.'

'It could happen. We're closer than you think.'

Augusta glanced back at the house, keen to leave. 'I should get going.'

'Yes, I suppose you should.'

They turned and walked towards the house.

'You do realise I shall have to tell your father that I've seen you?' said Aunt Lydia. 'He's my brother and family duty requires me to do so.'

Augusta gave an inward sigh. This had been the reason

she hadn't wanted to help Morris. But it was a risk she'd agreed to accept.

'Yes, I expected you would tell him,' she said. 'Although I can't imagine he'll be very interested. Especially if I'm spending my time with police officers.'

'And running a bookshop.'

'Yes, that as well. Which do you think he will be most disappointed about?'

'Such impertinence, Rebecca!'

'I call myself Augusta these days. It was the name I took on when I worked for British intelligence during the war.'

Aunt Lydia stopped. 'You worked for British intelligence? Doing what?'

'I was in Belgium. But that's all I'm allowed to tell you, I'm afraid.' Augusta smiled. 'It was nice to see you again, Aunt Lydia. I'm sorry it wasn't in happier circumstances.' She made her way to the door.

'British intelligence?' she heard her aunt say as she followed. 'Extraordinary!'

Chapter 8

As the maid led Augusta and Detective Inspector Morris to the entrance hall, another visitor arrived. He was a gentleman in his forties with tanned skin and a muscular build. His dark hair was flecked with silver and his eyes were a greyish blue like the colour of the sea.

'Oh.' He appeared embarrassed as he removed his hat. 'I didn't realise Lady Graywood had company.'

'We were just leaving,' said Morris. He held out his hand and introduced himself.

'Captain Pegwell,' said the visitor, giving Morris's hand a gruff shake.

'Captain Pegwell? I was planning to visit you today. This is excellent timing indeed.'

'Is it?'

'I realise you're here to visit Lady Graywood, but do you mind if we talk for a few minutes? This is Mrs Augusta Peel, Lady Graywood's niece. She's assisting with the investigation.'

'Niece? Assisting with the investigation? That seems like a strange setup.'

'Mrs Peel is an accomplished investigator.' Morris turned to the maid. 'Is there a room where we can speak to the captain for a few minutes?'

'I shall have to ask Lady Graywood, sir.'

Moments later, she returned with Aunt Lydia. 'What is the meaning of this, Detective? You can't simply jump on my visitors as soon as they set foot in my home!'

'I haven't jumped on him, my lady. I've merely requested to ask him a few questions about your husband. As second in command to Sir Graywood, Captain Pegwell will have some useful information for us, I'm sure.'

'Now is not the time, Detective.'

'I'm sorry, my lady, but I must insist on it. I was planning to call on Captain Pegwell today, so I can speak to him now and save myself the trouble of doing so later.'

Aunt Lydia looked at the captain. 'What do you think, Thomas?'

He shrugged. 'It makes sense to speak now. Even though I resent having my time commandeered in this manner.'

'Very well. Show them to Lord Graywood's study, Lottie.'

The maid nodded and they followed her to a small, comfortable room with a desk, bookshelves and worn leather chairs. A display cabinet near the window held vintage cricket balls, trophies and photographs of a cricket team. Half a dozen autographed cricket bats hung on the wall and an oil painting above the fireplace depicted a cricket match on a village green.

'I'm going to hazard a guess that Sir Graywood liked cricket,' said Morris.

'Yes, he did,' said Captain Pegwell, sinking into a leather buttoned armchair. He wore a smart black suit, but his boots were heavy and scruffy. 'By all accounts, he was a decent batsman. I can't say I care much for the game myself. He addressed Morris. 'So what do you want to ask me?' He drummed his large, tanned hands on the arms of the chair.

Morris took out his notebook. 'How long have you worked at Sir Graywood's shipping firm?'

'Three years. Before that, I served twenty-one years in what we now call the merchant navy. I was in command of several vessels during the war. We transported troops, food and coal whilst dodging the U-boats. I've lived to tell the tale but many good men have not.'

'Indeed,' said Morris. It sounds like you made a noble contribution to the war effort, Captain Pegwell.'

'I did my duty like every other man.'

'Were you Sir Graywood's second in command?'

'I don't like that description, it makes me sound more important than I am. I suppose I'm an assistant director of some sort. I just did whatever Graywood told me to. He was the one who made all the decisions.'

'Did Sir Graywood tell you about his plans to visit the West India Dock that night?'

'No, he never breathed a word of it to me. And I have absolutely no idea what he was doing there.'

'Can you make an educated guess?'

'There's no point. An educated guess will get us nowhere because it is just a guess. We need to know the facts, don't we? I really don't know what he was doing there.'

'He was found next to his ship, the *Colonia*. Perhaps he'd been on board? Checking the cargo, maybe?'

The captain lifted his hands, palms upturned. 'Who knows? Have you spoken to the *Colonia's* captain yet?'

'Not yet. Although I believe the Port of London police have.'

'The captain might know.'

'So you think it's possible he made arrangements with the captain without your knowledge?'

'Yes, entirely possible. He did a lot of things without my knowledge and I didn't mind that. He was the owner of the firm, so he could do what he liked. He consulted me when he needed to.'

'Perhaps there was something in the ship's cargo that interested him?'

'It may have done. But I wouldn't know.'

'The *Colonia* had just arrived from Antwerp, is that right?'

'That's right. She delivered a consignment of sugar from Paramaribo, Suriname to Antwerp. Graywood had made a deal with a Dutch sugar importer.'

'So before Antwerp, the ship had been in Suri…'

'Suriname. A country on the northeast coast of South America.'

'So what else was the ship carrying?'

'Tea and porcelain from China.'

'The *Colonia* went to China then Suriname?'

'That's right. It's very easy now we have the Panama Canal to sail from the Pacific to the Atlantic. Prior to that, it was a long, treacherous journey around Cape Horn, which is an archipelago off the southernmost tip of Chile. I'm sure you've heard of it. I can't impress on you enough the convenience of the Panama Canal, Detective. It reduces journey times by months.'

'All the better for trade and shipping, I imagine.'

'Yes. Much better for everyone.'

'So the *Colonia* has brought back a cargo of tea, porcelain and sugar?'

'That's right. Her journey began when she set off with a cargo of cotton for India earlier this year.'

'India as well? These ships get about, don't they?'

'It's what they're for, Detective.'

'Of course. Have you any idea who could have wanted Sir Graywood dead?'

'No, I can't think of anyone.'

'Lady Graywood suggested we could look at rival shipping firms. Are there any firms in particular you think we should consider?'

'All of them. None of them. I really don't know, Detective. It may be worth your while speaking to some gentlemen in those firms, but I should think it's unlikely any of them murdered Sir Graywood. Doing so would hardly help their own fortunes, would it? Graywood Shipping is a large company. Although we're finding it difficult to continue without Sir Graywood, we will soldier on. Anyone who thinks they can knock us off our perch by murdering Sir Graywood is deluded.' He got to his feet. 'Now, I'm happy to speak to you again, Detective, if there's anything else you need to know. But the purpose of my visit here today is personal, and I would appreciate being able to speak to Lady Graywood now in private. She's a dear friend of my wife's and I came here today to offer her some words of comfort.'

'I'll catch up with Captain Pegwell again,' said Morris after he and Augusta had left Aunt Lydia's house. 'We need to understand his relationship with Sir Graywood and I'd like to establish an alibi for him that night. Although I don't know what motive he has for murdering his employer, there's something rather fishy about him.'

'I expected him to be a little more upset and a little more helpful,' said Augusta.

'Exactly! I'm meeting Sergeant Finch from the Port of London police early tomorrow morning. He's going to show me the scene of the crime. Would you like to join us, Mrs Peel?'

'I certainly would.'

Chapter 9

'HOW WAS AUNT LYDIA?' FRED ASKED AUGUSTA WHEN SHE returned to the bookshop.

'Awful.'

'Oh dear. That bad?'

'She's clearly resentful that I left the family and lectured me on my duty. She also disapproves of the fact I work with the police and run a bookshop.'

Augusta sighed. The experience had left her with a heavy weight in her chest.

'I'm sorry to hear it,' said Fred.

'The encounter reminded me why I left my family. They haven't changed and they never will. I know I should feel some sympathy for my aunt because she's just been widowed for the second time. But it's difficult when she's rude. I know she's probably being rude because she's upset. And I suppose my sudden appearance must have surprised her.'

'You're making excuses for her behaviour,' said Fred. 'There's no need to. Perhaps she's usually a rude person anyway?'

'Maybe she is,' said Augusta.

'You mentioned you'd teach me how to repair books. There's no one in the shop at the moment. Do we have time now for a quick lesson?'

Augusta felt cheered by the idea. 'Yes, let's do that.'

In the workshop, books were piled on the table along the wall and sat in boxes under the window.

'There's quite a backlog, isn't there?' said Augusta.

'There's been a backlog for a while,' said Fred. 'We can make good money from all these books, so it's a shame to have them sitting here.'

'You're right, Fred. You have a good business mind.' Augusta began looking through the books. 'The trick is to find the ones which we can repair the quickest. We start with the simple repairs, then we can tackle the ones which need more work such as replacement covers and sewing in pages.' She pulled out a copy of *The Warden* by Anthony Trollope. 'This looks straightforward,' she said. 'The cover is intact. All it needs is a clean and we can apply some more gold leaf to the embossed lettering to brighten it up. The first thing you need to do, though, is check a book has all its pages. This one looks alright.' Augusta opened the book and a section of pages from the middle fell out and scattered across the floor.

Fred bent down to pick them up. 'Straightforward did you say, Augusta?'

She laughed. 'I was mistaken about that one.'

'It's just as they say,' said Fred, laying out the pages on the workbench. 'Never judge a book by its cover.'

Chapter 10

A LOW MIST HUNG OVER WEST INDIA DOCK EARLY THE following morning. The cry of seagulls carried across the water.

Augusta followed Detective Inspector Morris and Sergeant Finch along the cobbled quayside. She felt dwarfed by the great cranes and ships around her. Thick ropes tethered the ships to enormous mooring bollards and tracks were inlaid in the cobbles for the cranes to move along. There were carts and barrows and various pulley systems with chains and ropes which looked confusing to Augusta. She'd never visited London's docks before. They were hidden behind towering brick walls and access was limited to a few large gates with security guards.

'We don't have long,' said Sergeant Finch. 'This place will be filled with dockers before we know it.' He was an officious man with a thick brown moustache. The brim of his police helmet sat low over his eyes and the chin strap ran just below his mouth in a position which looked uncomfortable to Augusta.

'Here,' said Sergeant Finch, stopping and pointing at the cobbles. 'This is where Sir Graywood was found.'

Augusta peered at the ground. There was no sign that an awful atrocity had occurred here.

'The *Colonia*,' said Finch, pointing at the ship next to them. Augusta glanced up at the black steel hull. Above it, she could see the grimy white cabin and a tall black and red funnel. Further down the quayside, a wooden gangway leant against the hull at a steep angle.

'Do you know if Sir Graywood went onto the ship that night?' she asked.

'I can't say for certain. But I think the fact his body was found next to his ship indicates he was here to make an inspection of her one way or another,' said Finch.

'But why inspect his ship in the middle of the night?' asked Morris.

'That's the mystery.'

'If your chap, PC Buller, had come across Sir Graywood walking around here that night, what would he have done?'

'The protocol is to arrest any intruders and take them to the station,' said Finch. 'But as it was Sir Graywood, then PC Buller would have merely greeted him and asked if all was well.'

'Would PC Buller have thought it strange that Sir Graywood was here at night?'

'Undoubtedly. But Sir Graywood was entitled to do as he pleased.'

'Do you think the reason for his visit here that night could have been for illegal purposes?'

'Such as what?'

'Smuggling, Finch. Both you and I know it goes on.'

He shook his head. 'Not Sir Graywood. He would never have risked his reputation on something like that.'

'If he'd wanted to unload cargo from the ship at that hour,' said Augusta, 'could he have done it by himself?'

The sergeant laughed. 'By himself? Of course not. You need a gang of stevedores for that, Mrs Peel. Six or seven of them. You need a foreman, you need someone in the crane. You need men in the hold and you need men on the quayside. And it would be impossible to do in the dark. The man in the crane needs to be able to see the foreman so he can receive instructions on when to lower, lift, turn, and so on.'

'I'm assuming that's for large, heavy cargo,' said Augusta.

He laughed again. 'All cargo is large and heavy, Mrs Peel. Why else do you think we have these enormous cranes?'

'But if something was smuggled, then it could be small,' she said. 'It could be small enough to be hidden in the hold and carried on and off the ship. It could have been retrieved from the hold that night by someone walking onto the ship using the gangplank.'

'Smuggling?' said Finch. 'I refuse to consider the idea.'

'Why?' said Morris.

'Sir Graywood was not a smuggler!'

'Illegal activity could explain his death,' said Morris. 'If he was smuggling opium—'

'Graywood, an opium smuggler? You've got it all wrong, Detective.'

'Let's just consider it for argument's sake. If he was smuggling opium, then a gangster might have taken objection to it. We know how gangsters like to control the supply of drugs such as opium. It could explain Sir Graywood's death.'

Finch shook his head. 'If the Yard wants to consider

such fanciful ideas, then so be it. Here in the dockyard police, we like to take a simpler view.'

'So what do you think happened that night, Finch?'

'I don't know. But I do know it was a carefully planned attack. The assailant distracted PC Buller and his colleague PC Milton before setting upon Sir Graywood. The only answer to this is good old-fashioned police work. We're gathering statements from witnesses and have established that three vehicles were seen that night by the dockyard gates on West India Dock Road.'

'What sort of vehicles?'

'A van and two cars.'

'Did Sir Graywood arrive in one of them?'

'I don't know, but I assume so.'

'How did he get in?' asked Augusta.

'He would have had a key for the door in the gate.'

'Did he have a key on him when his body was found?'

Sergeant Finch paused for a moment, then gave her a sidelong glance.

'Now I come to think about it, he didn't.'

'That's interesting,' said Morris, writing something in his notebook.

Augusta heard the chatter of voices. She turned to see a group of men striding towards them. They wore flat caps and their trousers were tucked into heavy boots.

'Here they come,' said Finch. 'I told you we'd run out of time. We'd better get out of their way.'

Chapter 11

AUGUSTA FOLLOWED MORRIS AND FINCH BACK TOWARDS the dockyard gate. In no time at all, the cranes were moving and barrows and carts were being wheeled around on the quayside. Augusta walked cautiously, careful not to get in the way. Men shouted to each other, there was chatter and laughter too.

The dockers used hooks to manoeuvre heavy sacks of sugar onto trolleys. The work was clearly hard, but they moved quickly and effortlessly. Augusta felt the crunch of sugar grains beneath her feet as she passed them.

They paused with Sergeant Finch by the dockyard gate.

'I would like to have a look around Sir Graywood's office,' said Morris.

'There's no need. My men have searched the place already. Sir Graywood kept everything neat and orderly, and there are no clues whatsoever about what he was doing on the quayside that night.'

'All the same, I should like to take a look for myself.'

'Don't waste your time, Detective! The work is already done. Why duplicate our efforts?'

A pause followed as Morris considered this. 'Very well. Thank you for your time this morning, Finch. Please keep me informed and I'll do the same.'

They stepped through the door in the gate and a goods train passed over the railway bridge ahead of them.

'The scale of this place is quite extraordinary, isn't it?' said Morris. 'That train's just been loaded up in the sidings by the warehouses and now it's taking the cargo to somewhere on the other side of the country. In no time at all, rum from Jamaica can be served in a public house in Birmingham. I know this has been the way for many years, but the size of the enterprise still amazes me. There's St Katherine's dock, The West India and East India docks, Millwall, Surrey Commercial, the Royal Docks and Tilbury. Twenty-six miles of docks from the City of London out to the Thames Estuary. And all day and every day there are goods coming in and out, in and out. Right across the Empire and rest of the world. It's quite something, isn't it, Mrs Peel?'

'Yes, it is. It's a shame Sergeant Finch won't let us look in Sir Graywood's office.'

'Yes, that's a shame. There's little doubt he resents the Yard's involvement in this case, so it's probably an attempt to retain control of the investigation. I'll get in there sooner or later, I didn't wish to get into an argument with him just then in front of the dockers. I called on the captain of the Colonia yesterday to ask him about the ship's travels and cargo, but he couldn't tell me much more than Captain Pegwell. I suppose if the captain was involved in smuggling something, then he wasn't going to admit it to me, was he?'

'But why would someone as rich and successful as Sir Graywood get involved with smuggling?' asked Augusta.

'There's a good deal of money to be made from it. And some rich, successful people are still tempted by money. Greed, I suppose you could call it. Oh dear, I've just remembered I'm referring to your uncle, Mrs Peel. Please forgive me, I didn't intend to be disrespectful.'

'You haven't offended me at all, Detective. It's important to consider these things. What's the most lucrative thing to smuggle?'

'These days it's drugs, I'm afraid. It used to be tobacco, silk, spirits, that sort of thing. They fetch a good price on the black market. But drugs fetch much more.'

'Opium then?'

'Yes, although cocaine is becoming very popular now. Especially in the West End nightclubs. A lot of it arrives here from Germany. They have a rather liberal approach to the drug over there and I'm afraid we're suffering for it.'

'The *Colonia* called at India, China, Suriname and the Netherlands during her travels,' said Augusta. 'Perhaps she picked up opium from India?'

'She could have done. And dropped off some at China and then brought the rest back here. Although I must admit Sergeant Finch has a point. Can we really imagine Sir Graywood being caught up in something like that?'

'I don't know.'

'Hopefully we can find out. Thank you for accompanying me today, Mrs Peel. I shall keep you updated on the case. Any sign of Fisher yet?'

'Not yet.'

'Perhaps he's set up home on the south coast!' He chuckled. 'It's a bit of a shame because I was hoping he'd be around to watch our football match this evening.'

'Football match?'

'Yes, the Yard's team is up against the Flying Squad.

I'm not a regular player in the team, but they're short of numbers this evening and I used to play a lot as a young man. I'm looking forward to it.'

Augusta smiled. 'Good luck!'

Chapter 12

'I brought you chocolates, Lydia,' said Nancy Claydene, placing the fancy box on the table next to the sofa. It was tied with a silk bow. 'And grapes.' They were in a paper bag. Nancy set them down next to the chocolates and sat herself in an armchair. 'How are you?'

'I've been better,' said Lydia.

'Yes, I can imagine. You poor thing.' Nancy pushed her lower lip out in an expression of sympathy. 'Have you been getting enough rest?'

'Not really. It's difficult to rest when your husband has just been murdered.'

'I can imagine.'

'How can you imagine, Nancy? You've never been married.'

'No. But I've been in love. I know what that's like. And I know that if anything had ever happened to the man I loved, then I would have been beside myself with grief.' Nancy gave a sad sniff. 'Have the police caught anyone yet?'

'No. They're hopeless. There's the port police and there's Scotland Yard.'

'That sounds confusing. I thought the police were just the police.'

'That's what most people think, Nancy. Until they get caught up in something awful like this.'

'So awful.' Nancy shook her head and pushed her lower lip out even further. She was eighteen years younger than Lydia and had platinum bobbed hair and large dark eyes. Lydia thought her pretty in a chubby schoolgirl sort of way. Lydia came from a wealthy family and the two women had become friends while carrying out charitable duties for injured soldiers during the war.

'And you'll never guess who visited me yesterday with the police.'

'Rupert?'

'No. Why would it be Rupert? I told you that you'd never guess.'

'Oh, alright then. Who?'

'An estranged niece of mine. Lady Rebecca Buchanan. Although she calls herself Augusta Peel for some strange reason. She walked out on her family twenty years ago.'

'Walked out? Why?'

'Well, she's my brother Barnaby's third daughter. Unlike her sisters, she showed no sign of wishing to marry and settle down. To her credit, she was a clever girl and always did well in her lessons.'

'I think I know the rest of the story already,' said Nancy. 'She's one of those modern women who thinks her mind would be put to better use outside the home?'

'Yes. However, you don't know the full story, Nancy, so don't rush me. My brother and his wife made a silly mistake.'

'Oh dear. What did they do?'

'They organised Rebecca's marriage for her. They booked the wedding and invited all the guests. The chap was from the Montague-Barry family.'

'The Montague-Barrys? There's a lot of money in that family.'

'There is.'

'Although they do have that receding chin, which is quite unfortunate.'

'They do. The young chap in question was thoroughly decent, but he did have the chin. Anyway, Barnaby foolishly assumed Rebecca would go along with the wedding which was being arranged without her knowledge. She was at finishing school in Switzerland at the time.'

'And she rebelled?'

'I wish you wouldn't keep jumping ahead, Nancy, I'm about to explain everything. Rebecca did rebel, you're right. But not only did she do that, she came to London and had absolutely nothing to do with her family. The last I heard of her, that vulgar Lady Hereford had taken her under her wing.'

'Lady Hereford?' Nancy wrinkled her nose.

'My sentiments exactly. Anyway, Rebecca would have had to have found a job here because Barnaby cut her off completely. There was no money at all.'

'It seems they both behaved foolishly.'

'Yes, they did. I tried to talk some sense into him and told him he could have allowed Rebecca to choose her own husband. He was worried she would pick someone unsuitable, I suppose. We all thought she'd return one day with her tail between her legs. But no. She stayed away.'

'And she visited you yesterday?'

'Yes, Nancy. I'm just getting to that bit. It turns out she's a shopkeeper these days.'

'Oh dear.'

'It's a dreadful shame, isn't it?'

'What sort of shop?'

'It's a bookshop.'

'It could be worse. It could be a general store or something like that.'

'Very true. Anyway, not only does she keep a shop, but she also helps Scotland Yard.'

'What does she do there? Typing?'

'No. Apparently, she helps them investigate cases. And that's why she visited me yesterday. She accompanied a chap from Scotland Yard called Detective Inspector Morris. They asked me questions about Frederick which were quite unnecessary because I've already told the port police everything I know.'

'That's very strange. Your niece has never visited you before now and then she turns up with a Scotland Yard detective?'

'Yes. It seems she's only interested in me now that Frederick has died. A morbid curiosity, I suppose. And during the war, she worked for British Intelligence.'

'Really?'

'Yes. I asked her more about it, but she wasn't forthcoming. I suppose it's top secret, even now.'

'She sounds the adventurous sort. She would never have been able to do something like that during the war if she'd married the man your brother had in mind for her.'

'That's true. I don't suppose she has many regrets if she's doing the sort of thing she always wanted to. I just find it surprising she turned her back on the world she was born into.'

'She must have viewed it as a gilded cage.'

'She must have done. It was quite selfish of her to walk away as she did. I didn't love Noel, but I understood why I had to marry him. Such decisions are the reason the aristocracy endures. If we'd all married whoever we'd wanted to, then the bloodlines would have become diluted years ago. Not to mention all the lands and assets falling into the wrong hands.'

'The difference between you and your niece is that you understand how it ultimately works to your advantage,' said Nancy. 'Even if it means marrying someone you care little for.'

'Exactly, Nancy.'

'But it worked out well for you in the end, didn't it, Lydia? From what you've told me, Noel's death was shocking and untimely, but you had to endure a great deal at his hands.'

'It's never easy being married to a drinker.'

'And then you met Frederick and properly fell in love.'

'I did.' Lydia smiled at the recollection. 'His family was middle-class, though. My father wasn't particularly happy about it. But I was in my forties and he couldn't tell me what to do anymore.'

'You would never have known Frederick was middle-class,' said Nancy. 'He was perfectly at ease with all the lords and ladies around him, and fabulously rich, too. And he was a handsome viscount! You did very well for yourself, Lydia. Society ladies must have been very envious of you at the time of your wedding.'

Lydia paused for a moment. 'You speak rather highly of my husband,' she said.

Nancy's cheeks flushed red. 'Perhaps I spoke a little out of turn. I didn't mean to be quite so flattering. I suppose I'm trying to help you feel a bit better, Lydia. You must miss him very much.' Her face crumpled, and she dissolved into tears.

'Yes I do,' said Lydia. 'And it seems that you do, too.'

Chapter 13

'PHILIP'S BACK,' SAID FRED WHEN AUGUSTA GOT BACK TO the shop.

'Is he?' She felt a grin spread across her face. 'That's good news. Did he say much about his time in Worthing?'

'No.'

Augusta reasoned that if he'd rekindled his marriage, then he would have told Fred about it. Or would he?

'He said he had to come back for a new client who wants to visit him today,' said Fred.

'So that's the reason. He didn't come back because he missed us, then?'

'No. I don't think so.'

'Oh.' Augusta wanted to go up to his office and see him. But she also didn't want to appear too keen. She also liked the idea of Philip waiting in his office and hoping she would go and see him. But if he really wanted to see her, then surely he would come down?

Unsure what to do, Augusta fed some bird seed to Sparky.

'I thought you'd go up and see Philip,' said Fred.

'Do you think I should?'

'It's up to you, but he has been away for two weeks.'

'I thought he would come down here.'

'He did. But you were out.'

Augusta wondered if Philip had been disappointed that she'd been out. Then she realised how frivolous and foolish her thoughts were.

'I'll make some tea and take it up to him,' she said.

'Augusta!' Philip greeted her with a grin. 'Thank you for the tea, what a lovely thought. How have you been?'

Augusta sat across the desk from him. 'Well, thank you. You look well.' Philip had caught the sun a little and seemed relaxed.

'Thank you. I'm well.'

'How was your break?'

'Lovely.'

'Lovely?'

'Yes. Did you not want it to be lovely?'

'Oh yes. Yes, I did. I'm pleased you had a good time.' Augusta shifted in her chair, feeling uncomfortable.

'I hear you've been busy, Augusta. Fred told me all about your involvement with the Sir Graywood case.'

'Oh yes. It turns out he was my uncle. Not that I ever knew him.'

'Well, it was enough for Morris to ask you to help him, which is excellent news.'

'Talking of Morris, he'd like you to watch the Scotland Yard football team play the Flying Squad this evening.'

Philip groaned. 'I'd rather not. The Flying Squad were unbeaten last season. It could be embarrassing.'

'I got the impression Morris is looking forward to playing.'

'Morris is playing? Oh dear, we must be short of men. I would offer, but I'd be no use hobbling around with a dodgy leg and a walking stick. That said, I'd probably do better than Morris.' He laughed. 'Actually, that was a bit mean of me. Don't tell him I said that. Anyway, tell me all about Sir Graywood.'

Augusta told Philip what she'd learnt so far, pausing for sips of tea.

'He must have been up to no good,' said Philip once she'd finished. 'Why else would he have been there in the middle of the night?'

'I agree. Morris and I think he could have been smuggling something. Morris seems fairly sure it was drugs. Opium or cocaine. But the sergeant from the Port of London police refuses to consider it. He says Graywood would never have done such a thing.'

'How well did he know him?'

'I didn't get the chance to ask him.'

'And your aunt had no idea her husband was going to the dockyard that night.'

'No. He told her he would be staying overnight at his club on Pall Mall. I don't know why that didn't surprise her because their home is only about a ten-minute walk from the club.'

'Maybe it's not unusual for a gentleman of his status,' said Philip. 'Maybe they tell their wives they're going to stay over at the club because it gives them an opportunity to misbehave a little. Have lots to drink and play cards, maybe. The sort of thing their wives might disapprove of. I suppose they use it as an excuse for a little freedom. In Sir Graywood's case, it gave him the perfect opportunity to slink off to the dockyard without his wife knowing.'

'Sergeant Finch from the dockyard police said two cars and a van were seen near the dockyard gate that night,' said Augusta. 'We know Sir Graywood took a taxi from the club because the doorman hailed it for him. So one of those cars could have been the taxi.'

'Has Morris found the driver of that taxi yet?'

'Not yet,' said Augusta. 'And there's the van. Maybe that was needed to take the smuggled cargo away?'

'It could well have been. And if Sir Graywood went to the dockyard to unload the smuggled cargo, then perhaps he arranged for the van to be there,' said Philip. 'He had people helping him, didn't he? A man to drive the van and perhaps more to help unload the smuggled cargo.'

'Perhaps,' said Augusta. 'Or maybe I'm completely mistaken? Maybe he was there for another reason altogether, but I don't know what.'

'Do you think it's worth your while speaking to your aunt again?'

'Probably. Although I'm reluctant to. And I don't think she will confide in me. I think she dislikes me.'

'If she does dislike you, Augusta, it can only be because you decided to have nothing more to do with your family. She may have known you as a young girl, but she doesn't know you now.'

'Well, that's kind of you to try to reassure me, Philip. But I have to admit I don't like her either. She represents everything I ran away from. And she's going to mention our meeting to my father. I imagine he'll be disappointed to hear what I'm doing.'

'From what you've told me about your family, I expect he will be,' said Philip. 'But that's because he has narrow beliefs about what his daughter should do with her life. Try not to worry yourself about what he thinks of you. He doesn't know you, Augusta. And he's worse off for it.'

Augusta felt a lump in her throat. 'Thank you, Philip.'

Now was her moment to ask him how he had got on

with his wife during his stay on the south coast. Did they plan to reconcile?

The bell from the door downstairs interrupted her thoughts.

'That will be my client, Dr Lennox,' said Philip.

'Oh.' Augusta got to her feet. 'I shall leave you to it.'

'Thank you, Augusta. And thanks again for the tea.'

Chapter 14

FRED SHOWED AUGUSTA A BOOK HE'D BEEN WORKING ON when she returned to the shop.

'I've cleaned up *Sense and Sensibility*,' he said. 'It didn't need many repairs. What do you think?'

Augusta examined the book. It had a cornflower blue cloth cover and someone had written the initials "JB" with the year 1915 on the fly cover.

'It looks great, Fred. Well done.'

'Good enough to sell?'

'Yes, I think so.'

Fred smiled. 'I fixed my first book.'

'You can fix another one if you like and I can look after the shop.'

'Alright then.'

Augusta spent a pleasant hour serving customers and dusting and rearranging books on the shelves. As she worked, she thought about how well Philip looked. She could only assume he'd got on well with his wife during his stay in Worthing. Perhaps they'd agreed to make another go of their marriage. Maybe she was going to return to London with their son and dachshund dog.

If he hadn't got on well with his wife, then surely it would have showed in his face? He would have looked weary and sad. But instead, he seemed happy. They must have reconciled, and Augusta had to accept it.

'Just down here, Dr Lennox,' came Philip's voice from the top of the stairs. Augusta turned to see him descending slowly with his walking stick. The doctor followed patiently behind.

'And here's Mrs Peel,' said Philip. Augusta smiled and gave him a little wave.

The gentleman accompanying him was about forty-five. He wore a smart dark suit and had neat greying hair.

'It's a pleasure to meet you, Mrs Peel.' He held out his hand. He had a friendly face with expressive brown eyes. His handshake was warm and confident.

'It's a pleasure to meet you too, Dr Lennox.'

'What a lovely shop you have here.' He smiled broadly as he glanced around.

'Mrs Peel has repaired all the books you see here on these shelves,' said Philip.

'Really? What a skill you have, Mrs Peel.'

'Anyone can learn how to do it,' she said, her face feeling warm from the praise.

'Oh, I don't know about that,' said Dr Lennox. 'I suspect if I had a go, I'd make a right old dog's breakfast of it.'

Augusta laughed. 'It takes time to get good at it.'

'Even so, I wouldn't have the patience. And a canary!' He stepped over to Sparky's cage on the counter. 'He's completely adorable.'

'He's called Sparky,' said Augusta. 'He belongs to my friend Lady Hereford, but I look after him for her.'

'Like a nanny? A canary nanny?'

'I suppose so!' Augusta laughed again. Dr Lennox grinned and she liked the charming way his eyes crinkled at the edges.

'I've agreed to undertake some work for Dr Lennox,' said Philip.

'That's right,' said the doctor. 'I've heard good words about Mr Fisher, so I've had to call on his help. I've had a bit of trouble with some poison pen letters. Hopefully Fisher can get to the bottom of it.'

'You don't mind Mrs Peel knowing about the nature of your case?' Philip asked him.

'Not at all. A friend of yours is a friend of mine, and I can tell Mrs Peel is trustworthy.'

'She certainly is.'

'I'm sorry to hear someone's sending you unpleasant letters, Dr Lennox,' said Augusta.

'It's a bit of a nuisance,' he replied. 'A man can put up with four or five, I suppose. But when you reach a dozen, and then two dozen, it becomes rather exhausting.'

'How awful,' said Augusta. 'How long has it been going on for?'

'About six months. I reported it to the police and a helpful constable took an interest at the beginning. But when I returned with more letters, he grew tired of it. And the police are very busy, of course. They've got more important things to worry about than trying to find someone who's sending an old doctor like me some unpleasant letters. So that's when I decided a private detective might be able to help. I asked around and Mr Fisher came with a good recommendation.'

'Have you any idea who the sender could be?' asked Augusta.

'None whatsoever. I come across many people in the

course of my work. My guess is that it's a patient. But I can't work out which patient it could be.'

'Do you mind me asking what the letters say?'

'Well, they're generally filled with insults. And that's about the long and the short of it. I've clearly offended someone, and now they wish to write to me on a regular basis, calling me all sorts of names.'

'I'm sorry to hear it, Dr Lennox. I'm sure Mr Fisher will be able to help you.'

'That's what I'm hoping too. But that's enough about me. Please, tell me more about your lovely shop here, Mrs Peel.'

'I don't think there's much to say really,' said Augusta. 'I repair old books, then I sell them again.'

'This shop has such a nice feel to it. I just love old books. There's something about the smell of them, isn't there? I don't have a lot of time for reading, but when I do have time I adore sitting down with a good book.'

'What sort of books do you enjoy reading, Dr Lennox?'

'I love a good mystery. I enjoy the puzzle of working out who the murderer could be. I like to think that if I hadn't been a doctor, I would have been a detective. Although that really is just a romantic thought. In reality, my detective skills aren't very good at all. That's why I'm having to call upon Mr Fisher to help me identify the sender of these nasty letters. But when I read a good detective story, I can dream that I'm as good as the detectives at finding the clues and piecing them together.'

'But you're good at being a doctor.'

'Well, I'm not a man of many talents, but the ones I have are medical. So it makes sense that I chose the medical profession. Anyway, it's been absolutely delightful meeting you today, Mrs Peel. Mr Fisher tells me you're a good detective yourself.'

'Sometimes,' said Augusta. 'I try to help out where I can.'

Dr Lennox gave a loud laugh which startled her. 'I can always tell when someone's being overly modest! It's a characteristic I like in people. No one likes a braggart, do they? But I'm sure there's no need to hide your light under a bushel quite so much. From what Mr Fisher has told me, you're a very good detective indeed.'

Augusta blushed. 'Thank you Dr Lennox.'

'Don't thank me, thank him!' He laughed again and gestured at Philip. 'He's the one who's been singing your praises to me.'

'Thank you, Philip,' said Augusta, feeling embarrassed.

'Well, I've had a lovely time meeting you both today,' said the doctor. 'I do enjoy spending time with charming people. But I must get back to my surgery now. I've got a vicar with gout visiting me at one o'clock.'

'Hopefully you'll be able to find out who's been sending nasty letters to the doctor,' said Augusta once Dr Lennox had left.

'Yes, I hope so. He seems quite charming, but he's clearly upset someone. I shall have to do some investigating. He seemed very taken with you, Augusta.'

'Me?' She felt her face flush hot. 'No. He was just being friendly.'

'I don't know about that. He had a sparkle in his eye when he was speaking to you.'

'A sparkle? What does that mean? I didn't even notice it. You do talk some nonsense sometimes, Philip.'

'Lennox is an interesting chap.'

'Is he?' Augusta tried to sound not too interested.

'He was awarded the Victoria Cross for his service as a

doctor in the war. He rescued five injured men from no-man's land while under fire from the enemy.'

'He told you that?'

'Only when I pressed him. We had a conversation about the war and he's very modest about his contribution.'

'He doesn't sound modest if he told you he was awarded the Victoria Cross.'

'He has every right to boast about it, but he's a humble man. Along with being handsome, charming and brave. He has it all, doesn't he?'

'It takes a lot to impress me,' said Augusta, even though she was quietly impressed.

Philip laughed. 'Yes, it certainly does.'

Chapter 15

NANCY CLAYDENE BRUSHED THE COBWEB FROM HER HAIR and shuddered. She hated spiders.

She shone her torch around the attic, hoping she wouldn't see one. Perhaps there was a spider hanging from the rafters above her head, ready to jump down the back of her dress and...ugh! It didn't bear thinking about.

She made her way to the trunk, her skin itching. She undid the straps on the trunk and lifted its lid.

'Is everything alright up there, madam?' The maid's voice from the bottom of the stairs startled her.

'Yes. Everything's fine.'

'Anything I can help with?'

'No!' She scratched at her neck, trying to rid her skin of the crawling spider sensation. Then she put her hand into the trunk and pulled out the bundle of letters.

Lydia knew. She felt sure of it. She recalled now the expression on Lydia's face. As if she'd just found her out.

She would deny it, of course. But Lydia wouldn't believe her. Oh, what a horrible situation to get into!

Nancy rubbed her neck against her shoulder, trying to stop the itch.

The familiar sloped handwriting covered the papers in her hand. She would have to burn them now.

She took in a breath and made her way towards the staircase.

But no. She couldn't. Surely they were safe here in her attic? Surely no one would come looking for them?

She walked back to the trunk, wondering what to do. Destroy them or keep hold of them?

Chapter 16

'THERE'S UNFORTUNATE NEWS ABOUT DETECTIVE Inspector Morris,' Philip said to Augusta the following day.

'Oh no, what's happened?'

'He's broken his leg.'

'How?'

'He broke it in the football match yesterday evening. A nasty tackle from one of the Flying Squad sergeants apparently.'

'No! Is he alright?'

'He's laid up in St Thomas's Hospital and is going to be off work for some time.'

Augusta's heart sank. 'What a shame.'

'It's a big shame for Sir Graywood's case because it sounds like Morris had been making reasonable progress. He's slow and steady, Morris, but he's very determined and he always gets there in the end.'

'So who's working on the case now? Detective Sergeant Joyce?'

'No, it's been given to Detective Inspector Jenkins. I

know little about him other than he's recently joined the Yard from L Division.'

'And he's going to have to pick up where Morris left off,' said Augusta. 'Fortunately, Morris involved me in quite a lot of his work, so I'll call on Detective Inspector Jenkins and update him on how we've got on so far.'

Later that day, Augusta travelled by bus to Scotland Yard's stone and red brick building on the riverside at Westminster.

She had to wait some time to see Detective Inspector Jenkins. He eventually came to see her in the wood-panelled waiting room. He was a tall, lean man with a permanent scowl.

'I'm Mrs Augusta Peel,' she said. 'I've been working with Detective Inspector Morris on the investigation into Sir Graywood's murder.'

'Why?' The directness of his question seemed almost rude.

'Sir Graywood was my uncle.'

'Family members aren't usually asked to assist with murder cases, Mrs Peel.'

'I also happen to work as a private detective.'

'Oh, I see, that explains it. Well, I've had a look at the case, and I can see Morris has done some good work on it. I'll continue where he left off.'

'I met Lady Graywood with him and we also visited the scene of the crime and discussed it with Sergeant Finch from the Port of London police. He said—'

'Very good, Mrs Peel,' interrupted Jenkins. 'I've got this in hand now.'

'Don't you want to hear about the work we've done?'

'It's all in the file, Mrs Peel. Morris is very good with his records.'

'I was assisting Detective Inspector Morris. Would you like my continued help?'

'No, I don't think so, Mrs Peel. It's not common for the Yard to involve private detectives in our work. You've clearly been helpful, but your assistance is no longer required.'

Augusta felt her shoulders sink. Having learnt so much about the case, she couldn't bear the thought of not being involved anymore.

'I can help you if you need to speak to Lady Graywood. She's my aunt.'

'If that's needed, then I shall let you know, Mrs Peel. I don't envisage any difficulties speaking to Lady Graywood myself. It's been a pleasure meeting you. I'd better get on.'

'But Sir Graywood's office,' she said, as he turned away. 'Morris wanted to look in there, but Sergeant Finch told him there was no need. Morris really wanted to—'

'Thank you, Mrs Peel.'

She felt her jaw clench as she watched him stride away.

Chapter 17

AUGUSTA STILL FELT ANNOYED AS SHE STIRRED HER CUP OF cocoa in her kitchenette that evening. Every time she calmed down, the memory of Detective Inspector Jenkins's arrogant, dismissive manner enraged her again.

'It sounds awful to say it,' she said to Sparky as she walked into the living area. 'But I hope Jenkins fails.'

Sparky eyed her from his perch on the shade of the table lamp.

'I realise that a Scotland Yard detective is entitled to investigate a case however he likes,' continued Augusta. 'But to be rude about it is unnecessary. He looked at me as if I was little more than a bit of dirt on his shoe. I don't think he'd have looked at me that way if I'd been a man. In fact, I'm certain he wouldn't have. If I'd been a man, then he would've invited me into his office for a chat with a cigar and whisky. That's the way it goes, isn't it?'

Whether it was true or not, Augusta resolved to continue working on the case. If Jenkins was confident enough to solve it using Morris's notes, then she was going to use what she'd learnt so far. She sipped her cocoa and gave it some thought. Sparky flew from the lampshade to the dining table and preened his left wing. 'Rupert Graywood,' she said to the canary. 'That's who I'll call on tomorrow morning.'

Aunt Lydia had told Morris where Rupert lived. Augusta could recall the address: apartment five at Wentworth Mansions, Piccadilly.

She found the building on Arlington Street, near the Ritz Hotel. Wentworth Mansions was a Victorian apartment block with elegant bay windows and carved stone decoration.

Apartment five was on the second floor. Rupert Graywood's valet answered the door. He showed Augusta into the sitting room and told her Rupert would be with her shortly.

The comfortable room had pastel green walls and bookcases framed a gilded mirror above the fireplace. Plush pink sofas sat on either side of a mahogany coffee table with a vase of fresh flowers on it. Augusta looked out of the large bay window while she waited. The apartment overlooked smart townhouses on the opposite side of the street and a London Plane tree with russet brown leaves.

'Mrs Peel?'

She turned to see Rupert Graywood in the doorway. He wore a colourful silk housecoat with a paisley pattern. Beneath the housecoat he wore silk pyjamas striped in purple and green. His red hair was oiled and his cologne was an overpowering musky scent, as if he'd splashed too much on.

Augusta felt a little embarrassed that he was in his pyjamas but reasoned that perhaps he wore them all the time. 'Thank you for agreeing to see me, Mr Graywood.'

'Rupert, please.' He gestured for her to sit on one of the sofas and he sat on the other.

'Rupert,' she said. 'I suppose we're sort of related. By marriage.'

'Are we?'

'Lady Graywood is my father's sister.'

'Is she?' His eyebrows raised. 'So that makes us what? Sort of cousins? Stepcousins, I suppose, because she's my stepmother.'

'Yes, something like that. I must give you my condolences on the death of your father.'

'Thank you. I'm still coming to terms with it. That's normal, I suppose, isn't it? Cigarette?' He took a packet out of his housecoat pocket.

Augusta declined.

'Yes, I'm certainly still coming to terms with it,' said Rupert as he exhaled a cloud of smoke. 'What was he even doing there at that time? That's what I'd like to know.'

'I do some private detective work,' said Augusta.

'Do you? Really?'

'Yes. A Scotland Yard detective asked me to assist him.'

'No!'

'So we met with Aunt Lydia a few days ago and went to the scene of the crime.'

'Is that so?'

'So I've learnt a little bit about your father's death. But what he was doing there remains a mystery.'

'Complete mystery! I don't understand it. He was an old man! He should have been tucked up in bed. I hope we can find out what made him go down there that night.'

'He appears to have been checking on his ship,' said Augusta. Having just met Rupert, she felt wary about mentioning the idea his father had been involved with smuggling.

'He could have checked on his ship in the daytime, couldn't he?'

'Yes. And somehow the murderer knew he would be there that night, even though he didn't mention his plans to anyone.'

'Well, he must have mentioned them to someone, mustn't he?'

'He didn't tell your stepmother.'

'No. But that doesn't surprise me. He didn't really tell her anything. He kept business separate. And he certainly didn't tell me.'

'Why not?'

'Because he didn't involve me in anything. Even though I'm supposed to be working for the business.'

Augusta sensed some conflict between them. 'Did you get on with your father?' she asked.

'Get on? No. We never got on. I was a disappointment to him.'

'Why?'

'Oh, he had a great long list of reasons why.'

'But you worked for his shipping firm.'

'Yes. But only because I was his son. His only child who made it to adulthood, in fact. If there'd been others, then he would have employed them instead.'

'I'm sorry to hear your relationship with him wasn't good. When did you last see him?'

'About two weeks ago. He moved me to a different office. I had been working directly for him, but I made a slight mistake with one of his clients and he moved me to the billing office. It's so boring, I've not bothered turning up this week. In fact, I'm supposed to be there now.'

'How well do you know Captain Pegwell?' asked Augusta.

'Ugh, that man!'

'You don't like him?'

'He thinks he's better than everyone else just because he's sailed around the world ten times over. But he's just a sailor. That's all he is. An old salt.'

'Do you have any idea who could have killed your father?'

'No. Although if you were to force me to say, then my money's on Pegwell.'

'Why?'

'He can't be trusted. I think he's got something up his sleeve.'

'Such as what?'

'I don't know.'

'How did he get on with your father?'

'Fine. They got on well. But those are the people you have to watch, aren't they? They pretend to be your friend, then they stab you in the back.'

'You think Pegwell's like that?'

'Without a doubt.' He sighed out a puff of smoke. 'And I want to know what's in Father's will. I bet Lydia knows and she's not telling me. I hope he didn't leave everything to her because then I get nothing. Then when she dies, it all goes to her children. And what about me?' He rubbed his brow. 'I can't lose out. It's not fair!'

'Perhaps you could ask your stepmother about it?'

'I could, but we detest each other. I'm sorry, I realise she's your aunt, but she and I have never got on. I was fifteen when she married Father and she wanted nothing to do with me. Thank goodness I was away at school most of the time. Anyway, you're asking me lots of questions, Augusta. I don't mind but I'm wondering why. Are you going to do your private detective work on this?'

'Yes,' said Augusta. 'I am.'

'How exciting! I really want to know what Father was doing that night.'

'You mentioned you worked directly for him,' said Augusta. 'I don't suppose you have a key to his office, do you?'

'Yes, I've got keys.'

'Really?' Augusta felt pleasantly surprised. 'It would be useful to have a look in your father's office. That's if you don't mind.'

'Why should I mind? I'll fetch them for you.' Rupert stubbed out his cigarette in a large crystal ashtray on the coffee table and left the room. He returned a short while later with a bundle of keys. 'You'll return them to me once you've finished, won't you?'

'Of course.'

He showed her which keys worked in which door. 'The offices are on Lower Regent Street. About a ten minute walk from here. Hopefully you'll find something useful there. A note or a telegram maybe from the person he met. There must be something, mustn't there?'

'I hope so.'

Chapter 18

THE GRAYWOOD SHIPPING COMPANY OCCUPIED A GRAND cream stuccoed building on Lower Regent Street. Augusta stepped through the columned porch and into a large lobby dominated by a sweeping staircase. Large paintings of steamships hung on the walls and soft golden light spilled from ornate lamps.

'Can I help you, madam?' asked the smart young woman behind the polished mahogany desk. She had bobbed hair and red lips.

'Yes, my name's Mrs Peel and I'm Sir Graywood's niece. I have permission from his son Rupert to collect a few things from his office.'

'We have instructions from the police that no one's allowed into Sir Graywood's office. They've been searching it, you see.'

'The Port of London police or Scotland Yard?'

'I don't know which, I'm afraid. All I can do is tell you what they've told us.'

Augusta sighed. 'That's a shame, because Rupert

would really like me to collect a few things from the office which belong to him.'

'I expect he does. I'll tell you what I can do.' She leafed through the papers on her desk. 'One of them was in here yesterday and he left his card… oh yes, here we are. Detective Inspector Jenkins.'

Augusta felt disappointed to hear the name.

'And it says here he's from Scotland Yard. Alright then, what I'll do is telephone him now and see if he'll give you permission to go in there. Especially as it's for Rupert, Sir Graywood's son.'

Augusta already knew what Jenkins's answer would be. 'Oh no, it's alright. Please don't bother him.'

'I'm sure it's no trouble at all for him,' she said, picking up the telephone receiver. 'Especially when it comes to Sir Graywood's family.'

Augusta gritted her teeth as the woman asked the operator to put her through to Scotland Yard. Augusta prayed Jenkins was unavailable so he wouldn't find out she was trying to get into Sir Graywood's office.

To her disappointment, the receptionist got him on the telephone. 'Detective Inspector Jenkins? Oh good morning, sir. It's Miss Davis from Graywood Shipping. I have a Mrs Peel here, she's Sir Graywood's niece.' Augusta felt her toes curl with embarrassment. What would Jenkins be thinking now? 'She's requested to visit her uncle's office to collect some items which belong to his son, Rupert… I don't know which items, I'm afraid…would it be alright? I remember you saying nobody's allowed in there at the present time, so I thought I would telephone you to check. I see… Right, I'll tell her that then… Alright then, thank you, Detective Inspector Jenkins. Goodbye!'

She replaced the receiver and pulled a sorrowful face. 'He said no, I'm afraid.'

'So I gathered. Thank you, anyway.'

Chapter 19

'I REALLY DON'T LIKE DETECTIVE INSPECTOR JENKINS,' Augusta said to Philip later that day. They sat in the easy chairs in his office, and she had just told him about her visit to Rupert and Graywood Shipping. 'Why does he have to be so obstructive?'

'Because he likes to do things his way,' said Philip. 'And he doesn't want a lady detective poking her nose in.'

'Doesn't he realise how I can help?'

'Clearly not. But I wouldn't worry about him, Augusta. I'm sure you'll get into that office one way or another. Do you remember how we got into that German Generaloberst's office in Belgium during the war?'

'Yes. I suppose that was quite straightforward in the end.'

'Exactly. So you could pull off something similar at Graywood Shipping.'

'But the receptionist will recognise me.'

'Disguise yourself then, Augusta. You've done this sort of thing many times before.'

'I have. But it's rather nerve-wracking. I'm not sure I could pull it off again.'

'What are you hoping to find in the office?'

'A clue about what Sir Graywood was up to that night. I realise the police have already searched the office, but I thought it was odd when Sergeant Finch of the port police said they hadn't found anything. Surely there has to be something?'

'You'd think so. But if Sir Graywood was up to no good, then he will have kept it well hidden. That's just the sort of thing we were trained to find, Augusta. I'm afraid your average bobby from the port police doesn't receive that sort of training.'

'I'd rather speak to Aunt Lydia again than break into Sir Graywood's office,' said Augusta. 'Although it annoys me that Jenkins was there yesterday. What if he found a clue?'

'What if he did? Forget about Jenkins for now and think about what you can do.'

'I shall speak to Aunt Lydia again. I'll ask her about Sir Graywood's will.'

'That's brave of you Augusta, she wasn't particularly nice to you last time.'

'It has to be done.'

'Who are the main suspects at the moment, do you think?'

'Captain Pegwell is suspicious. He wasn't enormously helpful when Morris and I spoke to him. And neither did he seem too saddened by Sir Graywood's death. Rupert thinks he could be responsible.'

'Does he have evidence for that idea?'

'No. He just doesn't like him. That said, I don't think Rupert likes anyone very much. He strikes me as the sort of person who falls out with everyone.'

'Including his own father?'

'Yes.'

'So Rupert could be a suspect.'

'Yes, he could. He's quite concerned about the will, he wants to know if he's been left anything in it.'

'Which is understandable. But if your father has recently died in tragic circumstances, you don't tend to worry about the will too much.'

'Perhaps he's in need of money.'

'Perhaps he is. So Rupert could be a suspect, but we don't know the motive yet. Who else is there?'

'Aunt Lydia I suppose. But I don't see why she would murder her husband. What would she have to gain from it?'

'Perhaps you'll have more of an idea once you've spoken to her again.'

'And I'll need to speak to Captain Pegwell and Rupert too. I'm not looking forward to it.'

'Rupert's not so bad, is he? He's lent you the key to his father's office.'

'True. But can I trust him?'

Philip laughed. 'Surely you've learnt by now that you can't trust anyone, Augusta!'

His telephone rang and he got up to answer it. 'Fisher's Detective Agency... oh, hello Audrey. How are you?'

Audrey was Philip's wife. Augusta got up from her seat, waved a silent goodbye and went downstairs to her shop.

Chapter 20

'I MADE A SILLY MISTAKE WITH *LITTLE DORRIT*,' SAID FRED. 'And I blame Harriet.' He glanced at her and smiled.

'Me?' said Harriet. They stood in Augusta's workshop.

'Why are you blaming Harriet?' asked Augusta.

'Because I wanted to show her what I've learnt so far, and this copy of *Little Dorrit* appears to be in reasonably good condition. So I checked the pages, just as you told me to, Augusta. Then I repaired the spine with a little bit of glue. And I gave it a good clean. During this time, Harriet was telling me all about her grandmother's upcoming birthday celebrations. When I finished, I showed her the book. She had a look at it, then told me the last sixteen pages are missing.'

'Even though you checked them?' said Augusta.

'Yes. But I'd checked them while she was talking to me about her grandmother. So I got distracted and didn't check them properly enough.'

'So that's why it's all Harriet's fault.'

'Yes. I can't concentrate on two things at the same

time.' He grinned. 'But at least I got some practice, even if we can't sell this book.'

'That's a good way of looking at it, Fred,' said Augusta.

'Harriet's sorted all the books now so they're arranged in order of damage.' Fred pointed to the stacks of books on the table along the wall. 'The very worst one is *Vanity Fair*. Do you think it's got a chance at all?'

Augusta stepped over to the table and picked up the book. Its covers had fallen off, and the spine was coming apart.

'Yes, I think I can fix this one.'

'Really? I'm looking forward to watching you do it then.'

'Of course. I'll talk you through it as I go.'

A knock at the door interrupted them. It was Philip. 'You have a customer out here, Augusta.'

'Oh! I'm so sorry. We got distracted.'

She followed Philip into the shop where a familiar gentleman waited. 'Dr Lennox! I'm so sorry to keep you waiting.'

'Oh, please don't worry yourself about it, Mrs Peel. I've just dropped another letter in to Mr Fisher, and I thought I would call in again and have a good old browse of your books. But before I start, perhaps you'd like to point me towards some of your favourites? Perhaps a book which you can recommend to a dull old chap like me.'

Philip made his way upstairs to his office.

'Why do you describe yourself as dull and old, Dr Lennox?' asked Augusta.

'Because I'm not getting any younger and my job is rather boring these days.'

'And I can hardly agree with your description of dull when I've heard about your exploits during the war.'

'Mr Fisher mentioned them, did he? Oh dear, that's

embarrassing. It sounds like I've been bragging. I just did what any man would have done in my position. For those of us still here after those dreadful times, it's just luck. Wouldn't you say? You were in enemy territory yourself.'

Augusta nodded in agreement.

'And it's the guilt you feel afterwards,' he continued. 'When I think of the men who were lost... I shouldn't be here, really. But I'm happy that I am because I now have the opportunity to look around your wonderful shop.'

Augusta laughed. 'You speak about it in such flattering terms, Dr Lennox. There are plenty of second-hand bookshops in London. Have you visited the ones on Charing Cross Road?'

'Mrs Peel! Are you really trying to send me off to one of your competitors? I won't hear of it. And even though I'm sure there are plenty of other good second-hand bookshops in London, I can't imagine any of them being owned by someone as charming as yourself, Mrs Peel.'

Augusta felt her face flush hot. 'I see. Thank you.' She changed the subject. 'You asked me to recommend a book to you, Dr Lennox, and I would like to suggest a rather nice copy of *Wordsworth's Collected Poems*. It was in bad condition, and I spent some time on it.'

'I love Wordsworth's poems. Where might I find that one?'

'It's upstairs on the mezzanine floor. I shall fetch it for you.' Augusta crossed the shop floor and climbed the stairs. Dr Lennox followed her.

'Here it is,' she said, pulling the book from the shelf and handing it to him.

He gave a gasp. 'It almost looks as good as new, Mrs Peel!' He turned the book over in his hands. 'You've done a marvellous job with this. I wouldn't even know where to begin with a damaged book.'

'That's because you need to learn how to repair it. But if you did, then you'd be able to make it look much the same.'

'Oh, I doubt it. I don't have a steady hand.'

'You don't have a steady hand, and yet you're a doctor? Isn't it essential to have a steady hand in the medical profession?'

He gave a loud laugh. 'I suppose it's steady enough for my job. Although, with that said, I've had a few near misses. I shall have to tell you about them sometime.'

'Yes, you must.' As soon as she'd said the words, Augusta realised she was encouraging him.

Dr Lennox paused. Then he turned to her, holding her gaze.

'Forgive me if this sounds a little forward, Mrs Peel. I don't really know how to say this, but... I don't suppose you'd like to have dinner with me one evening, would you?'

Heat rushed through her face again, and she stumbled over her reply. 'Dinner?'

'Oh, I am sorry. I've caught you off guard, I can tell. That was rather rash of me, wasn't it? I apologise. I sometimes jump in and say these things with little thought. Please don't feel the need to respond. We can talk about Wordsworth's poems if you prefer.'

'No, it's fine,' said Augusta, feeling as flustered as Dr Lennox looked. 'It wasn't rash of you, it was just a little unexpected. But I think I should quite like to have dinner with you.'

'You would!' He grinned. 'Goodness. Well, that's marvellous indeed. Do you have a favourite restaurant?'

'No.' She desperately tried to think of one, but her mind felt empty. 'I don't. I'm ashamed to admit I don't dine out very often.'

'That's quite alright, never mind. Well, I have a few favourites. Perhaps I could choose one?'

'Yes, please do, Dr Lennox.'

'Very well. How about this Thursday?'

'Thursday would be nice.'

'I shall book a table at a delightful little Italian restaurant, Isola Bella, on Frith Street in Soho. Do you know it?'

'No, I don't. However, it sounds very nice.'

'It is. I'm really looking forward to it.' He grinned. 'Now, tell me how much I owe you for this book.'

'It's two shillings,' said Augusta. She felt unreasonable charging him for it. 'But you can accept it as a gift.'

'Absolutely not. You've put a lot of work into repairing it. Two shillings it is, Mrs Peel. And I'm looking forward to seeing you on Thursday evening.'

'Me too, Dr Lennox.'

'Are you alright, Augusta?' asked Fred as they closed the shop for the day.

'Yes, I'm fine. Why do you ask?'

'You look flushed and you seem fidgety. I wondered if you were coming down with something.'

'No, I'm not coming down with anything at all. I'm perfectly fine.'

But she didn't feel fine. She felt embarrassed, restless, excited, and nervous all at the same time. She struggled to believe that the handsome doctor had invited her out for dinner. She thought of the clothes hanging in her wardrobe at home and how none of them seemed suitable for an evening at a nice Italian restaurant.

Chapter 21

'HELLO REBECCA,' SAID AUNT LYDIA WHEN SHE RECEIVED Augusta in her burgundy and gold drawing room the following day. 'I suppose I should call you Augusta though, is that what you'd prefer?'

'Thank you, Aunt Lydia. I would prefer it.'

'Very well.' She cast a sideways glance at her friend who sat in one of the armchairs eating grapes. Her name was Nancy Claydene, and Aunt Lydia had introduced her as a close friend. She wore a silk black dress with a large bow at the neck and had blonde, bobbed hair and round cheeks.

'How are you, Aunt Lydia?' asked Augusta.

'As well as can be, under the circumstances.'

'I would like to discuss Rupert with you, if I may. I met him yesterday.'

'Did you? How was he?' Aunt Lydia's voice had a tone of disapproval.

'He seems well enough. He's worried about money.'

Aunt Lydia laughed. 'Yes, I expect he is! Did you hear that, Nancy? Rupert's worrying about money!'

Miss Claydene chuckled with her mouth full of grapes.

'It made me wonder about Sir Graywood's will,' said Augusta. 'Is Rupert a beneficiary in it?'

Aunt Lydia's nostrils flared. 'What an impertinent question!'

'I apologise. I didn't mean to be impertinent,' said Augusta. 'But in murder cases, the will of the deceased can play an important role. The matter of who benefits after their death can be crucial.'

'She's right,' said Miss Claydene. 'You'd be surprised how many people murder over money, Lydia.'

'I'm not discussing such affairs with a niece who has estranged herself from the family!' said Aunt Lydia. 'The matter is private.'

'If Rupert had inherited something, would he be aware by now?' asked Augusta.

Aunt Lydia rearranged the beads of black jet necklace. 'He might have done,' she said eventually.

Augusta assumed this meant Rupert had inherited nothing from his father. Had he murdered him hoping that some money would come his way?

Augusta decided to try the next difficult topic. She'd already offended her aunt, so she reasoned she couldn't make matters much worse for herself. 'No one seems to know why Sir Graywood was at the dock in the middle of the night,' she said. 'However, there are some suggestions he may have been caught up in some wrongdoing.'

'Wrongdoing? You do realise you're talking about your late uncle, Augusta?'

'Yes. And I thought it would be useful to tell you what people are saying.'

'People? What people?'

'Everyone. His murder has been the talk of London, Aunt Lydia.'

'And meanwhile, no one knows how I suffer!' She pulled out her black handkerchief and wiped her brow with it.

'People say he may have been smuggling something,' said Augusta. 'It could explain why he visited his ship in the middle of the night. He could have been unloading an illicit cargo.'

'Such as what?'

'I'm not sure,' said Augusta, cautious about upsetting her further.

'Opium,' said Miss Claydene.

'Opium?' Aunt Lydia turned on her friend. 'How dare you, Nancy!'

'I'm not suggesting he did it. But it's the sort of thing people smuggle.'

'I cannot believe anyone would even countenance the idea that my late husband was a smuggler! It's not fair on him. He's not here to defend himself.'

'I'm sure he wasn't,' said Miss Claydene. 'It's just what some people are saying, according to Mrs Peel. And it's only because he was there in the middle of the night. It's as if he had something to hide. That's what makes him look suspicious.'

Aunt Lydia gave a sniff. 'Poor Frederick. And it seems I'm the only person who is going to defend his reputation.'

'The police will find out the truth before long,' said Augusta. 'Someone somewhere knows what happened that night.'

'And the sooner they come forward, the better. I can't have Frederick's name besmirched like this. Your police friends had better get on and solve this, Augusta.'

'My police friends aren't working on it anymore. It's a gentleman called Detective Inspector Jenkins and he doesn't want me involved.'

'Why not?'

'I think he wants to manage the investigation his own way.'

'I see. Well, it's probably for the best, I thought it was rather strange that you were helping the Yard in the first place. I suppose you can get on now with running your bookshop.'

'I can still continue working on the case, Aunt Lydia.'

'Can you? How?'

'I'd like to look in Sir Graywood's office.'

'Why?'

'There might be clues there about who he met that night.'

'You think so? Well, maybe you should look there then.'

'I would, but Detective Inspector Jenkins won't let me. Perhaps you could speak to him about it?'

'Speak to him? I've never met the man. If he forbids it, then he clearly has a good reason.'

'If Mrs Peel is offering to help, then I think you should take her up on it, Lydia,' said Miss Claydene. 'The more minds working on this case, the better.'

Aunt Lydia sighed. 'If you think you can do something, Augusta, then go ahead. But if they've got a new chap at the Yard working on it, then I really don't see the point.'

Chapter 22

'I REMEMBERED YESTERDAY THAT A CHAP I TRAINED WITH went to work for the Port of London Authority police,' Philip told Augusta later that day. 'Robert Curtis. He's Sergeant Curtis now and based at Surrey Commercial Docks. I called on him in the evening and we had a drink at the Plume of Feathers in Greenwich. A very pleasant pub indeed. I asked him what he made of Sir Graywood's case. I hope you don't mind.'

'Why would I mind?' said Augusta.

'Because you're working on it, not me.'

'I don't mind.'

'Oh good. Anyway, I asked him about it and obviously he's not involved because he's south of the river. He thinks Graywood must have been involved with smuggling if he was at the dockyard in the middle of the night. He also thinks Pegwell must know more than he's letting on.'

'Does he know Captain Pegwell?'

'Not personally, but he tells me Pegwell is well known in the London dockyards for being a forthright character who always gets his own way. There are rumours he was involved in supplying the black market with bread and flour during the war, but nothing was proven. Apparently, Pegwell jumped at the opportunity to work for a powerful man like Graywood, and Graywood wanted him because of his years of experience as a seaman. Curtis says he finds it difficult to believe Pegwell knows nothing about Sir Graywood's activities on the night of his murder.'

'I really need to speak to him again, don't I?'

'Curtis tells me he can be found at the legendary Charlie Brown's.'

'Legendary? I've never heard of it.'

'It's actually a public house on the West India Dock Road called the Railway Tavern. The landlord's called Charlie Brown and he's been there almost thirty years. He's filled the place with treasures from his voyages around the world. It's a popular drinking den with workers and sailors who find themselves at the West India Docks.'

'So I need to go to Charlie Brown's,' said Augusta. It didn't sound like the sort of place many women visited. 'Everyone's going to look at me and wonder what I'm doing there, aren't they?'

'I can come with you if it helps,' said Philip. 'In fact, I insist on it. It's not the sort of place a lady should go unaccompanied.'

'Alright then. Thank you, Philip. When shall we go?'

'This evening? And let's hope Pegwell will be there.'

The Railway Tavern stood just a few yards from West India Dock railway station. It was an ornate four storey building occupying a wedge of land between the railway bridge and the road. It was topped with a tall ornate weathervane on a little domed roof. The pub's narrow sash windows were dulled with dust and smoke.

It was busy inside. Beyond the crowd of drinkers, Augusta could see dark wooden shelves crammed with exotic trinkets, vases, and statuettes. A long wooden bar stretched across the room, its shelves packed with time-worn bottles. The room was hot and smelt of tobacco, stale beer and sweat.

'Can you see Pegwell?' Philip asked Augusta. Their appearance had attracted a few glances. There were overseas sailors here, talking in languages Augusta didn't recognise. There were also rugged men in flat caps and shabby tweed jackets. They looked like the workers she'd seen in the dockyard.

'There,' she said, nodding to a table near the fireplace.

Captain Pegwell was sitting with a group of men. His shirt was tight around his broad shoulders. He was clearly good at sensing when he was being watched. Within a moment, his stormy blue eyes had met Augusta's, and he rose out of his seat, tankard in hand.

'Oh dear,' she said to Philip. 'He's seen us and he's coming over.'

'That's what we want, isn't it?'

Men moved out of the way for the captain as he approached.

'Mrs Peel?' He stood almost a foot taller than her. 'What brings you here?'

'I'd like to speak to you about my uncle if that's alright,' she said. 'This is my friend, Mr Fisher.'

Captain Pegwell shook his hand. 'Are you a copper?'

'I used to be,' said Philip. 'Do I look that obvious?'

The captain smiled. 'Very. Let's talk somewhere quieter.'

They followed him through a narrow door and up a staircase.

'How are you with your walking stick up these stairs, Fisher?' asked Pegwell.

'I can manage fine, thank you.'

He led them to a room with a grimy window which overlooked the railway line and dockyard beyond it. The sky was glowing orange with the setting sun.

In the room, four rickety oak chairs were placed around a table and a large map of the world hung above the fireplace.

Captain Pegwell placed his tankard on the table. 'Can I offer you both a drink?' he asked.

'Thank you,' said Augusta. 'A whisky and soda for me, please.'

'And me,' said Philip.

'Reynolds!' barked Captain Pegwell. To Augusta's surprise, a man immediately appeared in the doorway. 'Two whisky and sodas please.' He sat down and addressed Philip. 'A former copper, then. What do you do now?'

'I'm a private detective.'

'Trying to work out who had it in for Graywood, then?'

'I'm here to assist Mrs Peel. She wants to speak to you again about her uncle and I offered to accompany her here.'

'Very gentlemanly of you, Fisher.' The captain folded his large hands on the table and turned to Augusta. 'What would you like to ask me, Mrs Peel?'

'There are some suggestions my uncle could have been involved with smuggling. Do you think there's any truth in that?'

A smile played on the captain's lips. 'I don't know about the truth of it. But when you look at the facts, it's easy to suspect he was up to no good, isn't it?'

'Did you suspect before his death that he was caught up in something like that?'

He scratched his cheek and his fingernails raked on his stubble 'No,' he said. 'I never would've thought it. He never mentioned it and I never suspected it. But now, knowing what we know, I think he must have been. It's awful to hear myself saying it, really. He was a good man. But how else do you explain what he was doing there at that time? And the secrecy. He didn't breathe a word of it to anyone.'

'But his murderer knew he would be there,' said Philip.

'Well, yes. He clearly arranged something with the chap who murdered him.'

'Any idea who he could have been?'

The captain scowled. 'Obviously not. Otherwise I would have said something, wouldn't I?'

Reynolds returned with the drinks, placed them on the table, and left again.

'Do you think my uncle could have been smuggling drugs?' Augusta asked the captain.

'I really wouldn't know. I suppose it's the obvious contraband these days, isn't it? There's lots of money to be made from it. I wouldn't have said old Graywood would go in for that, but maybe he did.'

'A public house by the dockyard must attract some interesting characters,' said Philip. 'Have you heard talk of smuggling here, Captain Pegwell?'

The captain gave a wry smile, sat back in his chair and folded his arms. 'Just the sort of question I'd expect from a copper. Are you after names, Fisher?'

'No, I'm not asking for names. I'm just wondering how openly smuggling is discussed in a place like this.'

'Never heard a word of it myself. And anyone who came in here talking about such things would be a fool. If you're suggesting I've heard something, I can tell you now that I haven't. I've never smuggled anything in my entire career. Never seen anything smuggled. Never met a smuggler.'

Augusta recalled the claim he'd smuggled flour and bread during the war but chose not to mention it.

'I have a thought,' said Philip. 'Perhaps the person who murdered Sir Graywood knew he was receiving his illegal shipment. Maybe they killed him and stole it.'

The captain nodded. 'That could have happened.'

'So, do you see now why it would be useful to find out who could be involved in smuggling in the dockyard? That person could be a rival smuggler. Or a drug dealer, even. Someone who wanted that contraband.'

Captain Pegwell blew out a sigh. 'You're talking about serious criminality now, Fisher. It's something I know nothing about.'

'But do you agree it could have happened?'

'Yes, I agree it could have. People who smuggle and sell drugs are ruthless. If Graywood got caught up in drug smuggling, then the old fellow had no idea what danger he was putting himself in. If only I'd known about it and I could have warned him not to do it!' He shook his head. 'Very sad indeed.'

Chapter 23

Reynolds stepped into the room once Mrs Peel and Mr Fisher had left.

'Who were they, sir?' he asked.

Thomas Pegwell drained his tankard, then set it down heavily on the table. 'Mrs Peel is Graywood's niece,' he said. 'And the Fisher chap is a former copper. Works privately as a detective now. The two appear to be friends. Perhaps they're lovers. I don't know.'

'And what did they want?'

'They asked a lot of questions.'

'And you don't like people asking you questions, sir.'

'No, I don't. I've met Mrs Peel before. She was with a Scotland Yard detective at Lydia Graywood's house. That's Lady Graywood to you, Reynolds.'

'Yes, sir.'

'Lydia told me a strange story about Mrs Peel. It's not her real name, and she estranged herself from the family many years ago to avoid a marriage. Then she worked for British intelligence.'

Reynolds raised his eyebrows.

'All a bit peculiar, wouldn't you say, Reynolds?'

'I'd say it was peculiar, sir.'

Thomas got to his feet, knocking the table as he moved and sending the tankard and empty glasses toppling over. Reynolds picked them up.

'Speak to Finch, would you? And find out if they've been harassing him, too. I need to decide what I want to do about them.'

Chapter 24

'So it seems Captain Pegwell has never put a foot wrong in all his days,' said Philip after he and Augusta had left The Railway Tavern. 'Do you believe him?'

'No,' she said. 'I find it difficult to believe he's had a long career as a seaman without ever coming across any smuggling. I think it's difficult to say whether or not he knew about Sir Graywood's possible smuggling activities, though.'

'Yes, that's difficult to determine. We still don't know for sure that Graywood was smuggling anything. And it's impossible to know what Pegwell knew about it. But let's remember that Pegwell is going to portray himself as an innocent character because he doesn't want to be implicated in Sir Graywood's murder. For all we know, the two men could've had a terrible falling out and Pegwell went down to the dockyard that night and murdered Graywood in anger. I'm sorry to say it, Augusta, but I don't think our chat with Pegwell told us anything new, did it?'

'Which suggests to me he's keeping something from us,' said Augusta. 'He must know more than he's letting on. We need evidence, and I can't stop thinking about Sir Graywood's office. There must be some clues there.'

'I think it could be time you visited it, Augusta. If Rupert asks to have his keys back tomorrow, then you'll regret not making the most of the opportunity.'

He pulled a piece of paper from his pocket. 'I think we have time to visit this chap. I can only hope he's home and not doing the nightshift tonight.'

'Who is he?' asked Augusta.

'PC Buller, the constable who found Sir Graywood's body. Curtis knows him and gave me his address.'

Augusta grinned. 'Well done, Philip!'

Their route to the constable's house took them along busy Poplar High Street to Woodstock Road where a street of terraced houses overlooked a church. The churchyard appeared to be the only piece of green, open space in the area.

The sun was setting as they knocked on number fifteen. A tall young man with a soft, chubby face answered the door. He wore braces over his shirt and a pair of slippers.

'Constable Buller?' asked Philip.

'Erm, yes.'

'We're Mr Fisher and Mrs Peel. Private detectives. We'd like to speak to you about Sir Graywood if possible. Mrs Peel, here, was his niece.'

'Oh... He glanced at Augusta. 'I'm sorry about your loss, Mrs Peel.'

'I hope you don't mind us calling on you,' continued Philip. 'My friend, Robert Curtis, passed me your address.'

The constable gave a faint smile. 'Oh, Robbie. Yes. I

know Robbie.' The connection seemed to reassure him a little. 'Do, er... come in.'

A young smiling woman stood in the hallway, wiping her hands on her apron. 'This is my wife, Margaret,' said Constable Buller. He led them to a small, tidy front room. 'Do please take a seat. Any seat is fine. Actually, I'll take that side of the sofa because the spring's gone in it.'

The young man was nervous. Augusta smiled in an attempt to put him at ease.

'Tea?' asked Margaret once they were seated.

'Yes please,' said Augusta.

'Thank you,' said Philip. He turned to Constable Buller. 'I hear you were on watch at the dockyard when Sir Graywood was murdered,' said Philip.

'Yes.' He rubbed his brow. 'It was awful. And completely unexpected. The people who did it were clever. They got into one of the warehouses and made a noise. That was at three o'clock that morning. As soon as I heard it, I whistled for Constable Milton and we went in to have a look.'

'And found no one there?'

'No. We searched everywhere but they must have got out again as soon as they made the noise and attacked Sir Graywood while we were distracted. I hope you don't mind me asking, Mr Fisher, but are you helping with the investigation?'

'We're conducting our own investigation. As I've explained, Mrs Peel was Sir Graywood's niece. We both have detective experience, I was a detective inspector at Scotland Yard.'

'The Yard? Oh, I see, sir. So you know what you're doing.'

'Hopefully. If Mrs Peel and I come across any clues in

the course of our work, then we'll inform Detective Inspector Jenkins at the Yard.'

'And Sergeant Finch?'

'Finch?'

'He's my sergeant, sir.'

'Of course. We'll inform him too. There's no need to call me sir, I'm a private detective these days.'

'Alright, Mr Fisher.'

'So how long were you searching the warehouses for?'

'About an hour.'

'Before the sound was made in the warehouse, did you hear anything else unusual that night?'

'No.'

'Some cargo may have been unloaded from the *Colonia*. Did you hear anything like that?'

'No. I didn't hear anything being unloaded. If one of the cranes was used then it would have made a noise.'

'Did you hear any vehicles?'

'No.'

'If Sir Graywood planned to unload a cargo from the *Colonia* that night, then he would have needed a gang of dockers with him. Am I right?'

'Yes.'

'But you didn't see or hear anyone else there that night?'

'No.'

'It's possible Sir Graywood was murdered so the cargo could be stolen from him,' said Philip. 'That means another gang of men must have been in the dockyard that night.'

'If that's what happened, then I suppose there must have been.'

'So there could have been a lot of men there,' said

Philip. 'A gang to unload the cargo and a gang to steal the cargo. And there was also someone in a warehouse making a noise to distract you and your colleague. A van and two cars were also seen near the dockyard gates that night and they would have had drivers. And then there's the murderer himself. How many people is that, do you think?'

Constable Buller's lips moved as he thought. 'Erm… a dozen or so. Possibly more.'

'And yet you heard and saw nothing? No voices? No torchlights? No machinery or vehicle engines?'

'No. Just the noise in the warehouse. All those noises probably went on once we were inside it and couldn't hear them.'

'I see. Yes, that's possible.'

Mrs Buller brought in the tea tray and served tea. After she left, Augusta asked a question. 'How did Sir Graywood get into the dockyard?'

'I don't know,' said the constable, his tea cup poised beneath his mouth. 'He must have had a key.'

'Apparently no key was found on him.'

'I don't know, then.'

'How about the gang who stole the cargo? How did they get in?'

'I really can't say. I don't know,' said Constable Buller.

'You didn't let anyone in that night?'

'No! I would have said if I had.'

'Have you ever seen Sir Graywood at the dockyard in the middle of the night before?'

'No.'

'As nightwatchman there that night, what would you have done if you'd come across Sir Graywood and his gang?' asked Philip.

'Before he was murdered, you mean?'

'Let's imagine for a moment he wasn't murdered and you came across him unloading cargo from a ship in the middle of the night. What would you have done?'

'I'm sure Sir Graywood would have explained to me what he was doing and I would have let him get on with it.'

'You wouldn't have thought it suspicious?'

'No. Sir Graywood was a good man. I wouldn't have thought it was suspicious.'

'But you're a police constable, Buller. Wouldn't you have wondered what he was doing unloading cargo in the middle of the night? Wouldn't you have suspected there was something untoward going on?'

'No. I would have assumed Sir Graywood had a valid reason for being there. And even if he didn't, he wasn't the sort of chap I could question about such things. I would have got into trouble.'

The constable sipped his tea, placed his cup and saucer down on a little side table, then mopped his brow. It was obvious their questions had made him anxious.

Philip had clearly noticed his distress too. 'We'll leave you in peace now, Constable Buller. Thank you very much for agreeing to speak to us. You've been very helpful.'

'Have I?'

It was almost dark when they left the house.

'I don't really want to bother with the trains at this time of the evening,' said Philip. 'Let's hail a cab.'

'Sounds like a good idea. What did you make of Buller?'

'He strikes me as rather hapless. How could all those men have got into the dockyard without him noticing? And they somehow got away again before he and his colleague were finished in the warehouse? It all sounds rather too convenient to me.'

'I agree,' said Augusta. 'I don't think he told us the truth.'

Chapter 25

LADY HEREFORD VISITED THE SHOP THE FOLLOWING DAY.

'I keep expecting to read in the papers that they've caught Sir Graywood's murderer,' she said. 'But there's no mention of it at all. What's happening with it?'

'Not a great deal,' said Augusta. 'Scotland Yard is working on it, but I'm no longer assisting them because the detective in charge doesn't want me to.'

'Well, he's a silly man then,' said Lady Hereford. She fed a piece of apple to Sparky. 'He's taking his food very politely today. Have you been training him, Augusta?'

'No.'

'He's being very well-behaved. You could have lied and said 'yes' to take the credit for it.'

Augusta smiled. 'I didn't think of doing that.'

'Have you met your Aunt Lydia yet?'

'Oh yes. Twice.'

'Twice? How did it go?'

'She looks down on me because I run a bookshop and do detective work. But that was to be expected, I suppose.'

'So she's still a snob then.'

'She had a friend with her when I last visited. Miss Nancy Claydene. Have you come across her?'

The old lady rolled her eyes. 'She's an interesting character. She owns a chain of millinery shops called Claydenes.'

'Why is she an interesting character?'

'She's a lady with a reputation.'

'What sort of reputation?'

Lady Hereford laughed. 'Do I need to spell it out? Let's just say she's rather partial to other ladies' husbands. Lord Caulfield, Lord Manners, and even Lord Beresford.'

'Good grief,' said Augusta. 'Has she been the cause of divorces?'

'One or two. But you'd think it would be more. Some ladies put up with rather a lot from their husbands and choose to turn a blind eye to their infidelities. Especially if they're benefiting from the status and wealth their marriage gives them. I can tell by your expression, Augusta, that your mind's working rather hard on something now.'

'I'm naturally wondering if Nancy Claydene could have had an affair with Sir Graywood.'

'She's certainly the type.'

'But she seems to be good friends with Aunt Lydia, so maybe there was nothing between her and Sir Graywood.'

'I'm afraid that's sometimes how ladies like Nancy Claydene operate. They befriend the wife and build trust. And all the while, they're hoping for an introduction to the husband. And when that happens, she gets her claws into him.'

This description made Augusta feel protective towards Aunt Lydia. 'I really hope that didn't happen with Nancy and Sir Graywood,' she said.

'All you can do is make some enquiries, Augusta. I

imagine your aunt must be oblivious, otherwise she wouldn't still be friendly with Nancy. But servants usually know about these things, don't they? They don't miss much.'

Augusta heard Philip's footsteps on the stairs and he joined them.

'Hello Mr Fisher!' said Lady Hereford. 'How nice it is to see you again. Being kept busy?'

'Oh yes. How are you, Lady Hereford?'

'Very well. Happy to see Sparky in excellent form today.'

'Lady Hereford was just telling me about Lady Graywood's friend, Nancy Claydene,' said Augusta. 'We're wondering if she had an affair with Sir Graywood.'

'Really?'

'She's that kind of sort, I'm afraid,' said Lady Hereford. 'Anyway, I shall leave the pair of you to discuss it. I need to go on a little shopping trip and buy some more tea. I can't bear the tea at the hotel, I need to get my own.'

Philip held the shop door open so Lady Hereford's nurse could wheel her bath chair through it. Then he returned to Augusta at the counter. His brow was furrowed and his lips pressed together.

'Are you alright, Philip?' she asked.

'Yes, I'm fine. Although I've just had a telephone conversation with Dr Lennox.'

'Oh?' Augusta immediately felt guilty, as if she'd been caught out about something.

'Yes. He asked me to pass on a message to you. He says the table is booked at the restaurant and he's looking forward to seeing you tomorrow evening.'

'Ah yes.' She felt heat spread from her throat and across her chest. 'Yes. I see. Thank you for the message.'

Philip stared at her. 'You're going out for dinner with Dr Lennox?'

'Yes. He, erm, asked me a few days ago.'

'And you didn't mention it to me?'

'I completely forgot about it! I haven't given it any thought since he asked me.'

'I see.' His gaze wandered off to a bookshelf.

'It's nothing really,' said Augusta. 'It's just dinner. Is that alright?'

Philip turned back to her. 'Of course it's alright. Why shouldn't it be?'

'You seem to think I should have mentioned it to you.'

'Yes. Well, he's a client and you're a friend, so I thought you would. But it's fine. I hope you both have a lovely time.'

Philip's voice had a sadness to it which Augusta hadn't expected.

'Well, it's just—'

The bell on the shop's door tinkled as a police officer strode in.

Augusta sighed. Now she couldn't explain herself properly to Philip.

The man removed his helmet and marched towards them. His officious manner and thick brown moustache were familiar. It was Sergeant Finch of the Port of London Authority police.

Chapter 26

'MRS PEEL,' SAID SERGEANT FINCH. HE TURNED TO PHILIP. 'And I believe I'm addressing Mr Fisher, formerly of Scotland Yard.'

'That's right. How can we help?'

'I'm Sergeant Finch from the Port of London Authority police force. I hear you've been questioning one of my men, Mr Fisher.'

'Constable Buller?'

'That's the chap. I heard you gave him a cross examination.'

'Oh no,' said Philip. 'Just a few questions.'

'I'm trying to find out what happened to my uncle, you see,' said Augusta. 'And Mr Fisher is helping me.'

The Sergeant's moustache twitched. 'I see, Mrs Peel. But you asked him a lot of questions.'

'That's because there are a lot of things we need to know. There are many gaps in our knowledge and I'm trying to fill them in. To be honest with you, the Yard isn't doing much at all.'

'Well, I agree with that. I was rather relieved when that

Morris chap injured himself in the football accident. His replacement seems a little more on the ball, but the Yard needn't be getting involved at all. It's a matter for the Port of London Police, and we're quite capable of solving the case.'

'I'm pleased to hear it,' said Philip. 'What's your thought on the idea there may have been ten or twelve men in the dockyard that night?'

'That many?'

'Yes.' Philip explained his theory to Sergeant Finch. 'Where are those men now?' he added.

'They must be lying low.'

'In my view, there are an awful lot of men who know exactly what happened that night. And I'm baffled why none of them have been apprehended yet.'

'You'll have to ask the Yard,' said Sergeant Finch.

'I will. But surely you and your men must be asking questions in the local area? You're very familiar with the communities there. Someone's hiding these men. If they're all lying low, then there are people who know about it. The gang who assisted Sir Graywood with unloading the cargo that night would have been paid well for their efforts. There must be people who know who they are and they'll be envious of the money they received. The families of those men must have wondered why they went to work in the middle of the night.'

'Well, we're doing what we can to find them.'

'Presumably you have some regular informers in the area?'

'That's not for me to say.'

'Informers are the first people to speak to when something like this happens. All those men who were there that night! Someone must be ready to talk. Have you offered a reward?'

'The Port of London Authority Police Force can't afford a reward, Mr Fisher. That's something Scotland Yard will have to speak to the Home Office about.'

'Perhaps so. You have a detailed knowledge of the area and the people who live there, don't you?'

'I do.'

'The Yard doesn't have that knowledge. Surely if you can get someone to talk and you make a breakthrough, then it could be embarrassing for the Yard?'

'Are you encouraging me to undermine your former colleagues, Mr Fisher?'

'Yes, I think I might be. I like to do what I can to help them, but I also think some healthy competition from another police force keeps them on their toes.'

'Very well, Mr Fisher. I agree that perhaps there's a little more my men could be doing. And I'm happy to get on with it and keep you updated on our progress. On one condition.'

'That I don't get involved and speak to people myself?'

'You took the words right out of my mouth, Fisher. Yes.'

Sergeant Finch replaced his helmet and went on his way.

'We appear to have upset Constable Buller,' said Philip. 'He complained to his boss about us.'

'But you've sent him away again with a few things to think about,' said Augusta. 'You only forgot one thing.'

'Which is what?'

'To suggest he questions his own men. He can't do his job properly if they're not being honest with him.'

'Now that's true. Buller is holding something back.'

Augusta sighed. 'It's time to find the evidence that Sir Graywood was involved in smuggling that night. I've been putting it off, but I need to get into his office. And what I need are some large books.' She turned and opened the door to her workshop.

'What are you going to do with them, Augusta?' asked Philip.

'You'll see.'

Chapter 27

THE FOLLOWING MORNING, AUGUSTA STRODE IN THROUGH the doors of Graywood Shipping with a small parcel under her arm. She wore a flat cap, a brown work coat and spectacles.

'Delivery for Pegwell, Graywood Shipping,' she said in a gruff London accent.

The smart young woman behind the mahogany desk looked her up and down.

'Where's his office?' Augusta asked her.

'I can take it from you.' She held out a hand with neatly manicured nails.

'No, I've been told to take it up,' said Augusta, gripping the parcel protectively.

'Very well. Go up to the first floor, turn left, and it's the third door on the right.'

Augusta thanked her and marched off towards the staircase. She'd assumed that Captain Pegwell's office was close to Sir Graywood's.

The lady behind the desk called after her, 'Where's the boy?'

'He's come down with the flu,' said Augusta over her shoulder. She climbed the staircase two steps at a time and hoped the boy wouldn't put in an appearance later.

On the first floor, Augusta walked along the oak-panelled, carpeted corridor. Maps and more pictures of ships hung on the walls.

She reached the third door on the right. A bronze sign on the door said, "Captain Pegwell". She passed it and continued on, glancing at the names on the doors as she went.

There was no one around, but she could hear noises beyond the doors. The clatter of a typewriter and voices. People were nearby and someone could step out through a door at any moment and challenge her.

Just as she was losing hope, she reached Sir Graywood's office. It was the last door on the corridor. Her heart pounded in her ears as she fumbled with the keys in her pocket. They slipped a little in her gloved hands. Glancing about, she felt relieved to see no one in the corridor. She put the key into the lock and it opened with a satisfying click. Augusta slipped inside the room and quietly closed the door behind her. She locked it again.

A large mahogany desk stood in the centre of the room. Papers sat in piles, a brass inkstand held a feathered quill, and a crystal paperweight rested on documents. Bookshelves displayed leather-bound volumes and maritime ornaments. A large globe stood near an ornate drinks cabinet. The air in the room was stale, with a lingering smell of tobacco. A steady tick came from the gold maritime clock on the mantelpiece. It had two dials: one displaying the time, and the other was a barometer.

Augusta felt her stomach tighten. It would be easy for someone to discover her here. She had to work quickly. She estimated she had five or ten minutes before the woman at the front desk became suspicious.

She stepped over to the desk and looked at the papers laid out on it. Perhaps the police officers who'd searched the office had deemed these to be the most important. She leafed through them. They were mainly correspondence and details about the movement of ships.

The drawers of the desk were filled with more papers. Augusta guessed the police had already searched through them.

If there were any clues here about Sir Graywood's smuggling business, then where had he hidden them?

Augusta walked up to the bookshelves and pulled out some of the books to check they were not fake covers hiding papers. Then she looked behind the pictures on the walls, lifting them carefully to see if anything was attached to the rear of the frames. There was nothing.

Stooping down, she lifted the oriental rug in the centre of the room, checking for a floorboard that might have been recently disturbed. All the while, she could feel the ticking of the clock and knew she would be discovered here if she didn't hurry.

The floorboards were firmly fixed down. Augusta replaced the rug and examined the large globe on an ornate, polished pedestal. A semi-circular bracket was attached to its north and south poles, allowing it to turn. Looking closely, Augusta realised the equator had a ridge and the bracket had a hinge in it. The globe opened in two. But how? She turned it but couldn't find any obvious way of opening it.

Augusta checked the top where the bracket met the north pole. Then she checked the south pole. Her heart skipped as she saw a small switch. She pushed it and heard a faint click. The top of the globe jolted slightly, as if unlatched.

Cautiously, she opened the globe. Inside, at the bottom, was a small key. It looked like the sort of key for a trunk or chest, but Augusta couldn't see one in the room.

She picked up the key, lowered the top of the globe, and looked around the room again. Sir Graywood had hidden a small key in a globe. What did it open?

All the drawers in the desk were open. As were the cabinets in the room. The key she'd found had been deliberately hidden. The lock it opened would be difficult to find.

And Augusta didn't have the time to find it.

The woman behind the reception desk would surely raise the alarm at any moment. Augusta had already drawn her suspicion by telling her the usual delivery boy was unwell.

If she left now with the little key, she could return another time and look for the lock it opened. But if she delayed for much longer then she was bound to find herself in trouble.

With a sigh, Augusta headed for the door. She had found a key, but nothing else. Sir Graywood had done a good job of hiding his secrets.

She turned and gave the room one last glance before opening the door.

A picture of a ship caught her eye. It wasn't quite aligned with the others, hanging slightly lower on the wood-panelled wall. She recalled checking behind it and finding nothing of interest. But now it looked out of place. She hurriedly returned to it and looked behind it again.

In the wood panelling, at shoulder height, was a small lock. Augusta gave a quiet laugh of delight. There was room for her to fit her hand behind the picture and fit the key into the lock.

It clicked and the wood panelling opened inwards.

Chapter 28

THE WOOD PANEL DOOR REVEALED A SMALL, DARK ROOM. Augusta found a light switch just inside the door and flicked it on.

The little room was well-organised. It was lined with shelving and had space on the wall for a map of the world with pins placed in it. Beneath the map was a table and two chairs. Neat rows of boxes and files stood on the shelves.

Augusta took out a file and leafed through the papers in it. They detailed ship names, dates and destinations. The sort of information she expected Sir Graywood to have kept. But the secrecy of its location suggested to her it was connected with smuggling.

Other items on the shelves included a long pipe with a bowl at the end. It looked like an opium pipe to Augusta. Next to it was a blue glass hookah with an oriental design on it. And there were ornaments of nude figures which Sir Graywood had presumably deemed too risqué for display in his office or home.

A small glass bottle caught Augusta's eye. It was resting

on a piece of paper with "Post Office Telegram" written on the top of it. Augusta pulled out the telegram and saw it had been sent two weeks previously from Hamburg in Germany:

20 kilos despatched today. Acknowledge safe receipt.

Augusta examined the glass bottle. It was about three inches tall and an inch wide and filled with little white crystals. It was labelled in German: "Beruhigende Medizin". Augusta thought it meant soothing medicine which seemed an odd name. The label said the product had been manufactured in a factory in Hamburg. She recalled Detective Inspector Morris telling her that a lot of smuggled cocaine came from Germany.

Voices sounded beyond the door to the office. Augusta startled and put the telegram and bottle into her pocket. She quietly closed the little door to the room and locked it. Then she turned off the light and held her breath.

'She's not in here,' said a woman's voice. She sounded like the smart woman from the reception desk.

'She wouldn't be. The door was locked.' The voice belonged to Captain Pegwell.

'She could have broken in.'

'If you say so. Where's she got to, then?'

'She must be up here somewhere. I spoke to Agnes, and she hadn't delivered the parcel. I thought there was something funny about her when she turned up. Usually, it's a boy.'

'You were right to be suspicious. Remind me what she looked like,' said Pegwell.

'Flat cap, auburn hair, plain brown coat, spectacles.'

'And how old would you say she was?'

'Late thirties. Possibly forty. She looked familiar for some reason. Perhaps she's delivered parcels here before. But there's something not right about her. Just a moment… There's the parcel there. On the desk.'

Augusta felt her heart drop into her stomach. She had foolishly left it there.

'That's the parcel she came here to deliver?'

'It must be. Look, it's addressed to you. Captain Pegwell.'

'How did it get in here?'

'She must have given it to someone who brought it in here.'

'Who?'

'I don't know. Agnes said she hadn't seen her.'

Did they know about the secret room Augusta was hiding in? Would they look for the key inside the globe? Every muscle in Augusta's body was tense as she waited to hear more.

'We need to search the rest of the building,' said Pegwell.

Augusta gave a slow exhale when she heard them close and lock the door again. They would all be looking for her now. She had just a few minutes left.

She turned the light on again and had one last look around. She needed to gather more evidence. She took out the file which the bottle and telegram had stood next to. Inside it were some recent papers with details of shipments on. Augusta pulled them out, folded them up and put them in her pocket.

She was just about to leave when a brown envelope caught her eye. It had one word on the front: "Pegwell".

It was too big to put into a pocket. She opened her

coat, tucked it into the waistband of her skirt, then buttoned her coat again.

She left the little room, locked it, and made sure the picture was properly in position. Then she put the key back in the globe and made sure it clicked shut.

The parcel she'd left was no longer on the desk. Pegwell had taken it. Gritting her teeth with frustration, she tiptoed over to the door.

There was no sound beyond it. She slipped out into the corridor. Her mouth felt dry. If she was spotted now, she would be searched and the evidence she'd found would be taken from her.

She headed for a door she had noticed in the corridor on her way in. It was a little shabbier and plainer than the others and had no bronze sign on it. Augusta reasoned it led either to a storage cupboard or a service staircase. She prayed it was the latter.

Cautiously, she opened the door and was overjoyed when she saw daylight filling a cold, tiled stairwell. She dashed down the steps as quickly as her legs could take her.

At the bottom was a heavy door. It was locked, but the large key hung on a hook on the wall.

Voices sounded in the stairwell above her. Augusta grabbed the key from its hook, but it slipped from her gloved hands and fell to the stone floor with a loud clatter.

The voices grew louder. People were getting closer. Augusta pulled off her gloves, grabbed the key and pushed it into the lock. The handle was stiff, but she managed to turn it and push the door.

With a gasp of relief, she fell out into the yard at the back of the building. She pushed the door closed behind her.

The yard was enclosed by a wall about six feet high. Augusta glanced around, desperate to find a way out.

Ahead of her was a gap between the buildings which backed onto the yard. There had to be an alleyway there.

A row of dustbins stood against one wall. Augusta tried to move one, but it was too heavy. She tried another and managed to drag it four yards to the bit of wall by the alleyway. Carefully, yet hastily, she climbed onto the dustbin. It wobbled with her weight. She got a foothold and got on top of the wall just as the door behind her opened.

'Stop!' came a man's voice.

Augusta propelled herself off the wall and into the dingy, narrow alleyway. Pain shot through her right ankle as she landed. But she had to ignore it. She ran as fast as she could to the street ahead of her.

Chapter 29

'VERY INTERESTING INDEED,' SAID DETECTIVE INSPECTOR Morris as he examined the little bottle of white crystals. 'Beru... beri... berheru....'

'Beruhigende Medizin,' said Augusta. 'I think it translates as soothing medicine.'

'Is that so? And what does the rest of the label say?'

'It's from a factory in Hamburg.'

'Ah yes. I recognise the word Hamburg.'

Morris lay in his bed in St Thomas's Hospital with one leg raised up by a pulley system. He'd explained to Augusta and Philip that his leg had to remain in traction for six weeks.

Morris examined the telegram which Augusta had taken from Sir Graywood's office, as well as the papers detailing the shipments. Then he opened the envelope with the word "Pegwell" written on it.

Inside were five photographs which showed Captain Pegwell in a nightclub laughing with an attractive woman who sat on his lap.

'My guess is that's not Mrs Pegwell,' said Morris.

'It looks like Freda Buswell to me,' said Philip.

'Who's she?'

'An actress in the West End.'

'You know your West End actresses well, do you, Fisher?'

'Not especially. But I'm sure Audrey and I saw her in something a few years ago.'

Morris turned to Augusta. 'You've done some marvellous work here, Mrs Peel. But I'm not sure why you've brought it to me. As I've told you, I'm going to be out of action for the next couple of months.'

'We wanted to show you these before we give them to Jenkins,' she said. 'Do you think the soothing medicine could be cocaine?'

Morris examined the little bottle again. 'Yes, it could well be. I've come across these little bottles of drugs before. The telegram says twenty kilogrammes were despatched two weeks ago. How much is in this bottle? Two grammes. How many bottles of this size would make up twenty kilos? Let's see... fifty bottles would be one hundred grammes, then one hundred bottles would be—'

'Ten thousand,' said Augusta.

'I'm sorry?'

'Ten thousand bottles.'

'I see. Ten thousand little bottles like this.'

'It could be the cargo which was unloaded from the *Colonia* that night,' said Philip. 'The telegram was sent to Sir Graywood four days before his death. Four days is long enough to get a shipment from Hamburg to London via Antwerp.'

'But how did he get this little bottle and put it in his secret room?' asked Morris.

'Perhaps it was sent to him to test before he placed an order?' suggested Philip.

Morris nodded. 'That could explain it. Now, we need to be certain this is cocaine. Nurse!' He waved to a nurse who was walking through the ward. She came over to his bed.

'Yes, Mr Morris?'

'I'm doing a little police work from my bed. Could you please find someone who can take this bottle to Dr Russell's laboratory? I need him to test its contents for me as quickly as possible. Tell him it's from Detective Inspector Morris at Scotland Yard. He knows who I am, we work together from time to time.'

The nurse seemed bemused by this request. 'Very well.'

'Thank you, Nurse.'

'Very enterprising of you, Morris,' said Philip. 'I'm sorry we've got you doing work while you recover in your hospital bed.'

'Oh, I don't mind at all, Fisher. To be honest, I'm happy to do it. It's extremely boring lying here with one leg stuck in the air.'

'If you think about it,' said Augusta. 'Twenty kilogrammes isn't very heavy.'

'No, it's not,' said Philip.

'It's a lot of cocaine,' said Morris. 'And worth an excess of two thousand pounds, I'd say.'

'Yes, but it's small enough for one man to handle on his own, isn't it?' said Augusta. 'Twenty kilogrammes can easily be taken off a ship with no need for a gang of men and cranes.'

'That's an excellent point, Augusta,' said Philip. 'Ten thousand little bottles could have been placed in a few crates, none of them particularly heavy. It would have been very easy to handle them and hide them in the ship's hold.'

'Sir Graywood could have turned up on his own that night with a van,' said Augusta. 'He could have gone into the ship's hold and carried the crates out by himself. He could have loaded the crates into the van, then his attacker struck.'

'He murdered Graywood, then stole the van,' said Philip. 'So there needn't have been ten or twelve men there at all that night. Just Sir Graywood's attacker and another man to make a noise in the warehouse and distract the constable on patrol.'

'Or maybe the same man did both?' said Augusta. 'Perhaps only one other person was there in the dockyard with Sir Graywood that night.'

Morris picked up the photographs. 'Could it have been this man? Pegwell?'

'Sir Graywood clearly didn't trust him,' said Philip. 'That's why he had hidden some photographs he could blackmail him with if needed.'

'Perhaps he'd already threatened him,' said Augusta. 'Sir Graywood could have told Pegwell he had the photographs and threatened to show them to his wife if Pegwell didn't do his bidding.'

'Pegwell needs to be questioned,' said Morris. 'Leave this with me. I'll get a message to Jenkins at the Yard and ask him to pay me a visit. Oh look, here comes Dr Russell!'

A lean man with a loping gait approached them. He had wispy grey hair and wore a white coat.

'If I'd known you were here, Morris, I'd have paid you a visit sooner. What happened to the leg?'

'A nasty tackle from one of the Flying Squad's midfielders.'

'How unfortunate.'

'I'm going to be here for six weeks. But fortunately my friends here are keeping me busy.'

'That's why you sent me a bottle of cocaine?'

'It's confirmed then?' said Morris.

'Yes. Imported from Germany by the look of things.'

'Not imported, Russell. Smuggled. You've just helped confirm it.'

'Have I? Well, I'm glad I could be of use.'

Chapter 30

IT WAS LATE AFTERNOON WHEN AUGUSTA AND PHILIP returned to the shop.

Fred stood behind the counter, biting his lip.

'Is everything alright?' Augusta asked him.

'There's a man looking for you,' he said. 'A loud, large man. A bit angry and scary. Captain... I can't remember his name.' The shop bell above the door rang. 'Oh, here he is again.'

Augusta turned to see Captain Pegwell stride into the shop.

'Mrs Peel and Mr Fisher,' he said. 'I wasn't expecting to see the pair of you again so soon. I'm here to return something which belongs to Mrs Peel.'

He handed her the damaged copy of *Vanity Fair* which she had wrapped in brown paper to take into the shipping company.

'What makes you think it belongs to me?' she said.

'It's an old book and you make a living from repairing old books. It was left on Sir Graywood's desk after you tried to fool Miss Bletchley on the reception desk that you were a delivery person.'

'Exactly what are you accusing Mrs Peel of, Captain?' asked Philip.

'I'm accusing her of gaining unauthorised access to Sir Graywood's office.'

'You mean my uncle's office,' said Augusta. She reasoned there was little use in continuing to deny it. The police had the evidence she'd taken now.

'Oh, come now, Mrs Peel,' said Pegwell. 'You speak of him as if you were an affectionate family member. You never even met the man!'

'But he was married to my aunt and was therefore my uncle. I also had his son Rupert's permission to visit his office.'

'But not the permission of Scotland Yard.'

'They'll be grateful for my help.'

Captain Pegwell laughed. 'Will they, indeed?'

'Yes. Because it means they'll now be able to search the secret room I found.'

The captain's face fell and Augusta realised he had no knowledge of it. 'Secret room? What are you talking about, Mrs Peel?'

'My uncle kept detailed records of his smuggling activities there,' said Augusta.

His expression grew stormy. 'You're playing games with me, Mrs Peel. I worked with Sir Graywood for three years, and I never once encountered a secret room.'

'Perhaps he never entirely trusted you then, Captain Pegwell.'

'Of course he trusted me.'

'I'm not sure he did. In fact, I found evidence that he didn't trust you.'

'And what have you found?' His face paled.

'It's all been passed to Scotland Yard. They can deal with it now.'

He exhaled noisily through his nose. 'You've got no idea what you're messing with, Mrs Peel. You saw what happened to Sir Graywood.'

Philip stepped forward. 'Excuse me, but are you threatening Mrs Peel?'

'No. I'm warning her. I don't threaten ladies.'

'If you want to discuss this further, then I suggest you take it up with Detective Inspector Jenkins at the Yard,' said Philip. 'There's a lot he wants to discuss with you. You can help yourself by finding him before he comes to find you.'

Augusta noticed the captain's hands had balled into fists. He stared at Philip, and Augusta held her breath. Was he going to lash out?

'You do realise I could fell you with a single punch, Fisher?'

'Yes. But I don't advise you to.'

Pegwell turned to Augusta, sneered, then strode out of the shop.

'Pleasant man,' said Fred, after he'd left. 'I'll get on with some book repairs if that's alright, Augusta? I've nearly finished The Warden.'

'Have you? That's impressive. Yes, please do.'

He went into the workshop, and Philip checked his watch. 'I suppose you'll need to get ready soon, Augusta.'

'Ready?'

'For dinner with Dr Lennox.'

'Oh yes. That.'

'Are you looking forward to it?' he asked.

Augusta wasn't sure how enthusiastic she should sound. 'Yes. I suppose so. I like a nice Italian restaurant.'

'I expect Dr Lennox is looking forward to it a great

deal. I suppose it was quite obvious from the moment he stepped into this shop that he was quite taken with you, Augusta.'

'Was it? I didn't notice. Perhaps after an evening spent in my company, he might think differently. We might not get on at all.'

'Oh, I'm sure you'll get on absolutely fine. What lady wouldn't like to dine with a handsome doctor who also happens to be a war hero?'

'There's no need to be envious of Dr Lennox, Philip.'

'Envious?' He scowled. 'I'm not envious!'

'Good. There's no need to discuss him, then.' A pause followed, and Augusta sighed. 'Oh dear, why are we exchanging cross words about this? It shouldn't matter.'

'You're right.' Philip ran a hand over his brow. 'It shouldn't matter at all.'

'But for some reason, it does. You don't seem particularly happy that Dr Lennox has invited me out to dinner.'

'I'm indifferent to it. If he wants to ask you out for dinner, then that's his decision. And you've freely accepted and I'm sure you'll both have a nice evening.'

'You seem rather grumpy about it, Philip. And it's unfair because you have your wife and—'

'My wife?' He stared at her.

'Yes. You've just spent two weeks with her and she telephoned—'

'Audrey and I live separate lives.'

'But—'

The workshop door opened.

'Here it is!' said Fred, holding up the copy of The Warden. 'All finished!'

Augusta smiled. Her chest felt tight with all the things she wanted to say but couldn't. 'That was quick! It looks wonderful, Fred. Well done.'

Chapter 31

Soft amber lighting bathed the interior of the Isola Bella restaurant and reflected in the gold-framed mirrors. Couples sat in plush velvet chairs at tables dressed with crisp white linens.

Augusta and Dr Lennox sat at a table in the corner. A vase with a single red rose stood in the centre. The doctor was handsomely dressed in a smart dark suit and his cologne had a fresh, woody scent.

He gave Augusta a warm smile and his brown eyes creased at the edges. 'Thank you, Mrs Peel, for turning up,' he said. 'I worried you might change your mind.'

'Please call me Augusta.'

'And you must call me William.'

'Very well.' She smiled. 'Of course I was going to turn up. It would be awfully mean to change my mind and not tell you, wouldn't it?'

'Yes, but you never know with some people. It's happened to me before.'

'Then the lady in question should be ashamed of herself.'

They ordered red wine, then the waiter took their order.

'I can recommend the Chicken Milanese,' said William.

'Well, I shall have that, then,' said Augusta.

She sipped her wine and glanced around the restaurant. Most of the ladies wore dresses. Some with low necklines and spaghetti thin straps. Augusta felt underdressed in comparison. She'd chosen a navy silk blouse and a long navy skirt. In an attempt to brighten her face, she'd put on more rouge than usual and now worried it was a little too much.

William took a large gulp of wine, and she wondered if he did so because he was nervous. 'So when did you start repairing books?' he asked her.

'Before the war. I was on a bus and I found a copy of *Jane Eyre* left on the seat. It was in a poor state and I thought that was a dreadful shame.'

'You took pity on it?' said William with a smile.

'Yes. And I realised that if it could be repaired, then it could be read again. So, I borrowed a book about book repairing from a library.'

William threw his head back and laughed. 'A book about book repairing. How wonderful!'

Although Augusta could see the amusing side, she wasn't sure why he'd laughed so loudly. 'It was somewhere to start,' she said. 'And then I found a local bookbinder and asked if he could teach me his trade. I offered to pay him, but he refused. He was an elderly gentleman, and he told me he didn't have many years left. I thought that sounded rather miserable at the time, but it turned out to be true. When he died, he left me his workshop. It was in a basement in Bloomsbury, directly above the Piccadilly line between Kings Cross and Russell Square stations.'

'Goodness, was it quite noisy then?'

'Yes. I had to get used to the floor and walls shaking every three or four minutes.'

William let out another resounding laugh, and the couple at the neighbouring table glanced at him. Augusta felt a twinge of embarrassment.

'It's amazing what you can get used to, though,' she said. 'But after the war, I felt quite ready to hide away in a basement.'

William's face grew serious for a moment. 'Yes, I can understand what you mean by that. It was rather a lot to deal with, wasn't it?'

'Did you feel like hiding away too?'

'Not really. But I struggled with my patience when I returned. I'd spent so much time in those awful, muddy conditions tending to horrific injuries, and when I returned to my general practice, people visited me complaining about a sore toe. Looking back, I realise I was quite rude to some people. That was unkind of me. I reminded myself I had to show compassion to all my patients. It took a couple of years to feel like normal again. Whatever that is. And many others suffered far more than me, so I suppose I shouldn't be too hard on myself. Sometimes I wonder if I should have given up being a doctor altogether. Perhaps I could have made a living repairing books instead?'

'A book doctor,' said Augusta.

'That's right! A book doctor!' He laughed out loud again, his loudest laugh yet. Augusta wondered if she should tell him to quieten down. It was a small, intimate restaurant and most of its diners were now looking at their table.

She busied herself with her wine and told herself Dr Lennox was merely enjoying himself. She only wished he didn't laugh out loud so much.

As they ate, they discussed current affairs, books, plays and music they enjoyed. William was good company, but he drank a lot of wine. And the more he drank, the louder he got. After a couple of hours in his company, Augusta didn't feel as attracted to him as she had when they'd first met.

Chapter 32

Thomas Pegwell was summoned to Scotland Yard the following morning. He folded his arms and glared at the scowling lean man sitting opposite him.

'You're wasting your time,' said Thomas. 'I told that Morris chap everything I know.'

'Perhaps it's a waste of your time, Captain Pegwell,' said Detective Inspector Jenkins. 'But let me assure you it's a good use of my time.'

Thomas sneered. He didn't like the smug detective. And he didn't like the file of papers in front of him. What was in there? What did the detective know?

Jenkins pulled out an envelope and removed five photographs from it. He laid them out on the table so Thomas could see them.

He felt his shoulders slump. So Graywood hadn't been lying about the photographs. They existed.

'Can you tell me who this young lady is?' asked the detective.

Thomas gave the photographs a cursory glance. They'd been taken about three months ago in the Moonlight Lounge nightclub. How had he not noticed the photographer? He supposed Freda had been too much of a distraction.

He kept his breathing slow and calm as the thoughts raced through his mind.

'No idea,' he said.

'You have no idea who she is?' asked Jenkins. 'And yet that's clearly you in the photographs.'

Thomas gave the photographs another casual glance. 'That's not me.'

'It looks like you.'

'Maybe it does. But it's not me.'

'You're actually denying the photographs are of you, Captain Pegwell? This chap is the same age as you and he has the same build and the same facial features. And he's clearly enjoying the company of the young lady sitting on his lap.'

'Good for him.'

'And yet you claim it's not you?'

'You can't prove it is.'

Jenkins picked up one of the photographs and held it at arm's length, as if he were holding it next to Thomas and making a direct comparison. 'The similarity is remarkable,' he said. 'Do you have a twin brother?'

'No.'

Jenkins placed the photograph on the table again. 'I recognise this location as the Moonlight Lounge in Soho,' he said. 'The balustrade which runs around the edge of the dancefloor is quite distinctive, and I recognise it in the background of this photograph here.' He pointed at it with the nib of his pen. Captain Pegwell felt his heart race. He said nothing.

'And there are other people in these photographs,' he said. 'Some, if not all, of them are fairly easy to trace. We can ask them if they can identify the gentleman and lady in these pictures. In fact, we may have done so already.'

He gave a smug smile, sat back in his chair, and waited for Thomas to respond.

Thomas rubbed his chin. It was difficult to tell whether or not the detective was bluffing. How long had he had these photographs for? Who else had he spoken to?

'Where did you find these?' he asked.

'Ah ha, you're showing an interest in them,' said Jenkins. 'I can only assume that's because you're the gentleman pictured.'

'I don't recall them being taken.'

'But you recall visiting the Moonlight Lounge?'

'I've been there a few times.'

'And you recall meeting this young woman?'

'No.'

'That surprises me. Not only is she rather beautiful, she's also a successful theatre actress called Freda Buswell. My sources tell me she's currently performing in *Everlasting Summer* at the Empire Theatre. I'm surprised you don't recall meeting her, Captain Pegwell. Or maybe you're so accustomed to attractive young ladies sitting on your knee in the Moonlight Lounge that you can't tell between them?'

Anger surged through Captain Pegwell's chest. 'Why does this even matter? What does it have to do with anything?'

'This matters because of where the photographs were found.'

'And where were they found?'

'In Sir Graywood's possession.'

Mrs Peel must have found them and given them to Jenkins. If only he'd managed to catch her the previous day! His fists clenched with anger.

'Had you any idea Sir Graywood was in possession of these photographs?'

'No. Absolutely not. I didn't even know they'd been taken.'

'I can only guess Sir Graywood kept these photographs as a tool to bargain with. Perhaps he threatened to show them to your wife if you didn't do something he requested of you? Or perhaps he was blackmailing you?'

'I have no idea what he planned to do with them.'

'But you agree my theory makes sense? He kept these photographs to exert control over you. Why was that, do you think?'

'I've told you! I have no idea!'

'Nobody wants compromising photographs of themselves to get into the wrong hands, do they? And if that happens, then that person can become a problem. However, it's not a problem if they're silenced, is it? Sir Graywood couldn't do anything with those photographs once he was dead.'

'That's enough!' Thomas thumped the table. 'I don't claim to be a perfect man, Detective. But I'm not a murderer!'

Chapter 33

Augusta was feeding Sparky some birdseed when the telephone rang.

'Augusta, is that you?'

'Aunt Lydia?'

'Something awful has happened and I'm not allowed to tell the police.'

'What is it?'

'It's Rupert. He's been kidnapped.' Her breathing was fast and panicked.

'Kidnapped? When did this happen?'

'I received a telephone call late last night demanding a sum of ten thousand pounds. I haven't slept all night! The kidnapper has told me not to tell anyone about it. Especially the police. But I told him I don't have that sort of money. I really don't know what to do. I simply cannot find ten thousand pounds. I thought I could cope with this on my own and I've realised I can't. I need someone to help me. Will you help me, Augusta?'

'Of course.' She took in a breath and tried to remain

calm. 'Did the kidnapper reveal any information about himself?'

'No. Nothing.'

'How old did he sound?'

'I've no idea!'

'Did he have a young man's voice? Or an old man's voice?'

'Something in between. Now I think about it, I suppose his voice was quite young. Below the age of forty, perhaps. But I couldn't tell you anything more. I really don't know what to do.'

'Did the kidnapper give you a time and date for the drop-off of the money?'

'No, but he's going to telephone me again today. He told me I had to find the money and then he would telephone again with the details of where to take it.'

'Then we must wait for that next telephone call,' said Augusta.

'And do nothing more?'

'I realise the kidnapper says you mustn't tell the police, but you have to. Because when the kidnapper gets back in touch again with a time and place, then the police can make sure there's someone there to arrest him.'

'But he told me he would kill Rupert if I told the police!'

'Yes, that's a common thing for these people to say. He's issuing you with a threat because he doesn't want you to alert the police. But how is he going to know whether or not you've told the police?'

'He'll soon know when he sees them at the drop off point.'

'He won't see them there. They can be dressed in plain clothes and keep themselves hidden.'

'No, I can't involve them, Augusta. It's too risky. Oh, this is awful! I can't say Rupert is my favourite person, but I certainly don't want him to die. I have to look after him for Frederick!'

'I'm sure they won't want to harm Rupert,' said Augusta. 'They're just trying to extort money from you. I can speak to—'

'No! No one else can know.'

'Very well. Shall I come round?'

'If you could, Augusta, I would be very grateful. Thank you. And if I could just pay the kidnapper, then I would. I'd do anything to put a stop to this. But I don't have the money he's asking for.'

'You don't have ten thousand pounds?'

'No. Frederick died in debt. He left me nothing at all!'

Chapter 34

AUGUSTA TOOK A TAXI TO MAYFAIR AND AUNT LYDIA'S maid, Lottie, showed her into the drawing room.

'Oh Augusta! Thank you for coming to see me!' Aunt Lydia was pale. Her eyes were rimmed with red and there were dark circles beneath them. The lean black cat watched them from the hearthrug.

Augusta sat beside her aunt and took her hand. 'I know you won't like what I'm going to say, Aunt Lydia, but I'm afraid I shall insist on it. You have to tell the police about the kidnapping.'

'Oh, but I can't!' she wailed.

'Yes, you can. The kidnapper wants money. He doesn't want to kill Rupert. If the police are involved, then they can be extremely tactful about it, and the kidnapper will have no idea they've been consulted. Scotland Yard deal with cases like this all the time. They know exactly what to do.'

'Do they?'

'Yes.' Although Augusta couldn't be certain it was true, she felt confident that it was.

'I suppose they know better than I do about this sort of thing,' said her aunt. 'But it's very hard to agree to it when someone is threatening a member of your family. Although Rupert is my stepson and I'm not sure that he ever cared for me very much, I have a duty to protect him, don't I? Especially now that his father isn't here. I'll never forgive myself if something happens to him!' She broke out into tears.

'I can speak to someone at Scotland Yard for you,' said Augusta. 'Then, as soon as the kidnapper telephones with the details of where to take the money, we can inform them. You don't even have to speak to the police directly. I could do it for you. And then you're not actually telling the police, are you? I am.'

Aunt Lydia nodded and wiped her nose as she tried to control her sobs.

Augusta heard the telephone ring in the hallway. Moments later, Lottie knocked and entered. 'There's someone on the telephone for you, my lady.'

Aunt Lydia jumped to her feet. 'Did he give a name?'

The maid shook her head.

Aunt Lydia grasped Augusta's hand. 'Come with me.' Her aunt's palm felt cold and clammy. She walked with her into the entrance hall and to a wood-panelled recess below the main staircase where the telephone was fixed to the wall. A console table and a velvet-covered stool were placed beneath it. Aunt Lydia remained standing as she picked up the receiver and spoke.

'Hello?'

Augusta watched her aunt's face. Her eyes widened as she listened. Then she grabbed a pen and a little notepad on the console table and scribbled down some notes. 'But I've told you already, I don't have ten thousand pounds. I don't know where to get it from. My husband died with enormous debts. How's Rupert?' She paused to listen. 'Can I speak to him? How do I know he's with you?' She paused again. 'No, I don't have anyone I can borrow the money from, I don't have any means of paying them back... Sell the house? I couldn't do that... I don't understand why you're doing this to me! Can't you understand I've suffered enough? But you must understand, I don't have the—' She stopped, then stared at the receiver in her hand. 'He's ended the call.'

She sighed and replaced the receiver on the telephone. Then she picked up the notepad she had scrawled on. 'He says I'm to put the money in a bag and leave it next to the Statue of Achilles in Hyde Park at ten o'clock tomorrow. He told me I must be alone when I bring it so there can't be any police nearby. Even if they're wearing plain clothes. He tells me Rupert is fine. But he would say that, wouldn't he? I don't know where he's keeping him or whether he's even giving him enough food and drink.'

'I'm sure he will be. He wants to keep him alive, doesn't he?'

'Oh, I hope so. He'd better not harm him! Oh, this is interminable.'

Augusta took her hand and helped her back to the sitting room.

Lottie brought in tea.

'I want to telephone Nancy,' said Aunt Lydia. 'But I'm not supposed to tell anyone about the kidnap.'

Augusta recalled Lady Hereford's low opinion of Nancy Claydene. It was unlikely Miss Claydene was a genuine friend, and she felt the need to protect her aunt from her. 'Hopefully this will all be resolved tomorrow and you can tell her then,' she said.

Had Miss Claydene had an affair with Sir Graywood? Augusta thought it possible Lottie might know.

'Oh drat!' She looked down to where she'd purposefully spilt some tea onto her lap. It was hotter than she'd realised and was already soaking through her skirt and burning her leg. She put down her cup and saucer and jumped to her feet.

'I'll call the maid,' said Aunt Lydia.

'No need,' said Augusta. 'I'll go myself.'

She dashed out into the entrance hall and found a staircase leading downstairs to the kitchen. Lottie was making her way up.

'Please can I have a quick word?' Augusta whispered to her.

Lottie nodded, wide-eyed.

'Where can we speak?'

'The study is nearby.'

Augusta followed her to the cosy room with its cricketing memorabilia, then closed the door.

'You'll probably think I'm rather deceptive,' Augusta whispered. 'But I have to confess I spilled some tea on myself to speak with you without Lady Graywood present.'

Lottie looked worried. 'What do you want to speak to me about?'

'Well, it's a rather delicate matter, I'm afraid. But I'm trying to work out who murdered my uncle. And to understand that, I need to understand who he associated with. Obviously, my aunt has told me what she knows. But I also realise there may be some relationships which she doesn't know about. It's crucial that I find everyone who had something to do with him. If I ask you a question about my uncle, do you promise to keep the matter confidential? I only ask you to do this because I worry about my aunt's feelings being hurt. She's a grieving widow, and I'm sure you can understand there are some conversations which would be too difficult to have with her at this time.'

Lottie wiped her hands on her apron. 'I'd like to do whatever I can to help, madam. I can't say I know much about Sir Graywood's affairs, though.'

'How well do you know Nancy Claydene?'

'Not very well.'

'Do you know if Sir Graywood knew her well?'

Lottie glanced out of the window and bit her lip, as if considering how to answer. A pause followed and Augusta admired a blue and white porcelain plate on the wall as she waited.

But Lottie was unforthcoming. Eventually, Augusta prompted her. 'I only ask because I've heard some... stories. It could just be gossip. But I would really like to know if there's any truth to it.'

'Maybe all I've heard is gossip too,' said Lottie. 'But there has been talk that Sir Graywood and Miss Claydene were friendly.'

'And do you understand that to mean an affair?'

'I suppose so. But I don't like to think about it. Because he's dead and poor Lady Graywood is grieving. It's not fair on her.'

'No, it's not fair on her. And that's why I want to have this conversation in private with you, Lottie. It's not something I particularly want to consider myself, but perhaps the affair is something the police can question Miss Claydene about.'

'Don't tell them it was me who told you!'

'No, I promise I won't. Hopefully, the police will encourage Miss Claydene to confirm the affair.'

'But she wouldn't have murdered him, I know that. I don't know her very well, but she wouldn't have done something like that.'

'No, I don't think so either.' She said this to reassure the maid.

'I don't want to get anyone into trouble!'

'No one will know it was you. Thank you, Lottie, for your help.'

'I feel bad for Lady Graywood. Miss Claydene comes here pretending to be her friend, and she knows nothing about it.'

'She's having a difficult time. And that's why I want to ensure the murderer is caught. Hopefully, Lady Graywood will get some comfort when justice is served.'

Chapter 35

AUGUSTA RETURNED TO HER SHOP AND IMMEDIATELY called on Philip in his office.

'Rupert Graywood has been kidnapped,' she said.

His jaw dropped. 'Kidnapped? When?'

'Yesterday at some point. Aunt Lydia received a telephone call from the kidnapper late last night and told her not to tell anyone. But fortunately she telephoned me and I've just visited her. I've persuaded her to involve the police.'

'Well done, Augusta.'

'I told her Scotland Yard would help, so I really hope they will do.'

'I'll make sure they do. I'll speak to Jenkins about it as this could be connected to Sir Graywood's family. Has Jenkins thanked you yet for discovering the secret room in Graywood's office?'

'No. But I don't expect him to. He's probably embarrassed he didn't discover it himself.'

'True.' Philip sat back in his chair. 'So who's decided to

kidnap Rupert Graywood? I wonder if it's the same person who murdered his father and stole the shipment of cocaine.'

'But why kidnap him?'

'Money?'

'Why do they need money if they've just stolen cocaine worth two thousand pounds?'

'What ransom amount are they demanding?'

'Ten thousand pounds.'

'A larger amount. They're clearly greedy.'

'It still doesn't make sense. They could have stolen Sir Graywood's cocaine without murdering him.'

'Perhaps they didn't plan to murder him, but he saw their face that night?'

'Maybe,' said Augusta. 'Or was the attack a failed attempt to kidnap him?'

'A robbery and attempted kidnap.' Philip gave this some thought. 'Are you thinking he struggled too much, and they silenced him instead?'

'It's a possibility, isn't it? Otherwise, I don't understand why Sir Graywood would be murdered and then his son kidnapped ten days later. And if it's the same man, then he might murder Rupert if he doesn't get his money. He's already murdered once, he presumably has few qualms about doing it again.'

'We're dealing with someone extremely unpleasant here. If it's a drug gangster, they can be ruthless. Morris has more knowledge of them than I do. It might be worth having a conversation with him about possible suspects.'

'We might not need to. If the Yard can spring a trap when the kidnapper arrives to collect the money, then he'll be caught.'

'Good point, Augusta. Has your aunt arranged anything with him yet?'

'She has to leave the money in a bag by the statue of Achilles in Hyde Park at ten o'clock tomorrow. But she doesn't have the money. Apparently her husband died leaving debts.'

'Despite his supposed wealth and success?' said Philip.

'It seems so. Graywood Shipping wasn't doing as well as we'd all thought. It explains why he turned to the lucrative trade of drug smuggling.'

'Yes, it does. And it seems the kidnapper is unaware Sir Graywood's family is in debt.'

'Apparently, he suggested to my aunt that she sell her house.'

Philip shook his head. 'What an unpleasant man. I'm confident the Yard will catch him. The Yard has a reserve of forged notes which can be used for dropping off the money. The kidnapper won't even have time to check them before he's apprehended.'

'But the police must do it carefully, Aunt Lydia's terrified that Rupert will be harmed.'

'They will be careful, Augusta. They're experienced with this sort of thing. I'll telephone Jenkins now.'

'Thank you, Philip. And please tell them how frightened my aunt is. She really doesn't want Rupert to be harmed.'

'I will.'

Augusta got up from her seat. She was nearly at the door when Philip spoke again. 'How did you get on with the doctor?'

'He was fine.' Augusta felt her face warm up.

'Just fine?'

'Yes. Fine.'

'So, does that mean you enjoyed your evening?'

'Yes, I did. It was a very nice restaurant.'

'Well, that's nice to hear,' said Philip. 'Do you think you'll go out for dinner with him again?'

'Possibly.'

'I see.' He picked up his telephone receiver. 'I should phone Jenkins.'

Chapter 36

AUGUSTA DESCENDED THE STAIRS TO HER SHOP, HOPEFUL that Scotland Yard would apprehend Rupert's kidnapper and find Rupert safe and sound.

A young man stood in the shop, glancing around at the bookshelves.

'Can I help you?' she asked. As he turned, she recognised his soft, chubby face. 'Constable Buller?' He was dressed in a grey suit and fidgeted with a hat in his hands.

'Hello, Mrs Peel. I've come er… to tell you something.'

'Oh. What is it?'

'I, er… wasn't quite truthful before and I've been feeling terrible about it.'

'Alright. Do you mind if I ask Mr Fisher to join us so you can tell him too?'

'I'd rather just speak to you for now, Mrs Peel.'

'Alright. We can talk in my workshop.'

Fred was in there, counting the pages of *Barchester Towers* by Anthony Trollope. 'I'll look after the shop for you, Augusta,' he said with a smile. He left the room.

'You have a lot of books in here,' said Constable Buller, eying the stack of books on the table by the wall.

'We do.' Augusta smiled. 'What do you want to tell me, Constable?'

'I want to be honest,' he said. 'But I'm worried I'll lose my job.'

Augusta wasn't sure how to respond. If the constable was about to tell her something which could solve Sir Graywood's murder, then it was going to be difficult to keep it confidential.

'So your account of that night is untruthful?' she asked.

He nodded.

'Do you know who murdered Sir Graywood?'

'No. I don't know who did it.'

'So why have you lied about what happened?'

'Because I was paid,' said Buller.

'By who?'

He scratched the back of his neck. 'Sir Graywood.'

'I see.' Augusta smiled. 'For a moment, I thought you were going to tell me you helped the murderer.'

'No! No, I don't know who attacked him and I would never have had anything to do with harming Sir Graywood. I liked him.'

'Because he paid you money?'

Buller nodded, then slumped onto a stool and put his hat on the workbench. 'I've been wanting to tell someone for a long time. I knew it was wrong, but…'

'Why did Sir Graywood pay you money?'

'To turn a blind eye.'

'So your story about someone making a noise in the warehouse that night to distract you, is that true?'

'No.'

'There was no noise in the warehouse. Sir Graywood paid us to wait in the station while he was there.'

'Us?'

'Oh dear.' He put his head in his hands.

'Did he also pay your colleague, Constable Milton?'

He nodded.

'Was it the first time he paid you? Or had it happened before?'

Constable Buller removed his hands from his face and sighed. 'It happened a few times. Nine or ten, maybe.'

'So whenever Sir Graywood needed to unload an illicit shipment, he paid you both to look the other way?'

'Yes.'

'And you heard and saw nothing that night because you were in the station?'

'Yes. We were told to be there between three and four. We had tea and biscuits and went out again about half-past four. Then I couldn't believe it when I found him. That bit is true. My account of when I found him is all true, I swear it.' He fixed her gaze, his eyes wide and imploring.

'I believe you,' said Augusta. 'And you're doing a good thing by telling me the truth.'

'Well, I thought I had to tell someone. Sir Graywood wasn't supposed to die that night. And if I'm lying about some of it, then it's going to make it harder to catch the killer, isn't it?'

'Yes, it is. Did you see Sir Graywood at all that evening?'

'Yes, I let him in.'

'At the gate?'

He nodded.

'Did he have a van with him?'

'He drove it in. I don't know where he kept it, but he used it each time.'

'And that was the last you saw of him?'

'Yes. He drove the van up to the *Colonia* and Milton

and I then had to go and wait in the station. We're both going to be in a lot of trouble over this.'

'Sir Graywood was a powerful man,' said Augusta. 'It would have been difficult to say no to him.'

'Yes it would.'

'Impossible even. You accepted his money and agreed to his wishes because you were frightened about what would happen if you didn't.'

'Yes, that's right, Mrs Peel!'

'So there's your defence. I'm not sure you'll be able to keep your job if you tell your sergeant the truth. However, you were put in such a difficult position by Sir Graywood that you had no choice but to do his bidding.'

'I'll tell Sergeant Finch that.'

'Good. I hope he's understanding.'

'I hope so too.'

'Thank you for coming here to tell me what happened,' said Augusta. 'It can't have been easy for you.'

'Oh, it wasn't.' He took in a deep breath. 'But whatever happens now, I feel better for this. I feel better that I've finally told someone what I did.'

Chapter 37

'WHO'S HE?' SAID FRED AFTER CONSTABLE BULLER HAD left.

'He's the poor man who found Sir Graywood's body,' said Augusta.

'How awful.'

'He's just told me a little bit more information about the case and I'm wondering what to do with it.' She felt reluctant to inform Scotland Yard yet because she didn't want to get Buller into trouble. Hopefully Buller would confess all to Sergeant Finch and the matter would be dealt with from there. 'In the meantime, have you heard of Claydenes?' she asked Fred.

'The hat shops? Yes, I know them. My mother loves them.'

'Do you know where the branches are?'

'There's one on Bond Street. And I think there's one on Baker Street, too. There are more, but I can't remember where they are.'

'Thank you Fred. I want to speak to the owner, Nancy Claydene. I think she had an affair with Sir Graywood.'

Fred raised his eyebrows. 'Is that so?'

Claydenes on Baker Street had a smart red frontage with colourful hats displayed in the window. Inside, hats adorned with pastel ribbons, feathers, and flowers were displayed in polished mahogany cabinets. A middle-aged saleswoman in a grey dress was assisting a customer when Augusta entered.

'I will be with you in one moment, madam,' she said.

'Thank you. I would like to speak with Miss Claydene.'

'She's in the Bond Street shop today.'

Augusta thanked her and made the ten-minute walk to the other shop.

Claydenes on Bond Street was the same as the previous store but a little larger. Miss Claydene's platinum bobbed hair was hard to miss as she rearranged some hatpins on the counter. She wore a fashionable low-waisted scarlet dress with a pleated skirt.

'Mrs Peel? This is a surprise. What brings you here?' She looked a little older than Augusta but dressed much younger. It made Augusta wonder if she should wear more fashionable styles.

'I'd like to ask you about the Graywoods, if possible.'

Miss Claydene pulled a grimace. 'I see.'

'How long have you known them?'

'Let's talk out the back.' She called over to a young woman polishing the cabinets. 'Polly! Can you keep an eye on things for me?'

Polly nodded and Augusta followed Miss Claydene into a cosy little room with velvet chairs and fabric draped on the walls. It was much nicer than Augusta's draughty workshop.

Augusta declined a cigarette from Miss Claydene and made herself comfortable.

'I've known them since the war,' said Miss Claydene, after she'd puffed a cloud of smoke into the centre of the room. 'Lydia and I met when we were selling flags for wounded soldiers. Do you remember those?'

'I do.'

'And I met Frederick, I mean Sir Graywood, a little while after that. I knew him properly for about two years.'

'Knew him properly?'

'Yes. As a friend.'

'How well did you know him?'

'Not as well as I know Lydia. He was always kept busy with his work. And understandably so. He was incredibly successful, wasn't he? I can only guess the person who did this to him was jealous of his success.'

'Did he mention anyone who was jealous of his success?'

'No, he never mentioned it. He was a humble man. But there are people who can't bear it when someone's successful, aren't there?'

'So you think someone murdered him because they were jealous of him?'

'Yes. But I suppose he must have been causing a problem for them. Perhaps his company stole business from them and they decided they couldn't be successful until he was out of the way...' She tailed off and gave a sniff. 'Oh, I'm sorry. It's just so terribly sad!' She rested her cigarette in a shell-shaped ashtray and pulled a handkerchief out of her bag.

'You seem quite upset by his death,' said Augusta.

'Upset?' She wiped her eyes. 'Of course I'm upset! Everyone will miss him very much. Especially Lydia. She doesn't deserve this!'

'Have you ever heard the gossip about you and Sir Graywood?'

Nancy Claydene blinked a few times, then cleared her throat. 'I'm sorry? Gossip? You don't strike me as a gossip, Mrs Peel.'

'I'm not, as a rule. But occasionally there can be truth in it.'

'I wouldn't believe any gossip.'

'Are you interested in what people have been saying?'

'No, I'm not interested at all. People who gossip are jealous.' She dried her eyes and picked up her cigarette again.

Augusta took in a breath and prepared herself for a strong reaction. 'Some people say you and Sir Graywood had an affair,' she said.

Nancy Claydene said nothing. Her lips thinned, and she stared into the middle distance. The pause was uncomfortable, but Augusta remained silent and waited for Miss Claydene to speak.

'There's absolutely no truth in that whatsoever.' Her voice cracked. 'Lydia is my best friend. I would never dream of doing such a thing to her.'

'So where did the gossip come from?'

'I don't know.' Her voice cracked again. Then a sob took over. 'Oh dear, what a mess!' She stubbed out her cigarette and cried into her handkerchief.

Polly, the shop assistant, peered into the room. She stared at Miss Claydene for a moment, then looked at Augusta. 'Is everything alright?'

'Sort of,' said Augusta. She reached out to Miss Claydene and rested a consoling hand on her arm.

'I'll make some tea,' said Polly.

Miss Claydene began to recover herself and removed her handkerchief from her face. Her black eyeliner was smudged around her eyes. 'It's been very difficult not being able to grieve for him,' she said. 'Lydia can grieve all she likes! Even though she fell out of love with him many years ago. But me? I've had to remain silent on the matter. I've had to comfort her even though I was the one in love with him!' She gave another sob. 'No one has any idea how I'm feeling. It's been torment! He was an adorable man. I've still kept all his letters and when I feel sad, I go up to the attic and read them. I thought about destroying them but I couldn't bring myself to do it.'

She pulled a little mirror out of her handbag and sighed at her smudged makeup. Augusta sat patiently as Miss Claydene rubbed at her face and reapplied some lipstick and rouge. 'I suppose I feel a little better now I've spoken about it.' She turned to Augusta. 'But you won't tell anyone, will you? No one must ever find out! And if Lydia finds out, she'll be completely distraught. I would lose a friend!'

'If your affair had nothing to do with Sir Graywood's death, then my aunt needn't know about it at all,' said Augusta.

'It had nothing to do with it! Nothing at all.'

'Could a former lover of yours have jealously attacked Sir Graywood?'

She gasped. 'Former lover? What sort of lady do you think I am, Mrs Peel?'

Polly brought in the tea and their conversation came to an end.

Chapter 38

'GOODNESS AUGUSTA,' SAID PHILIP LATER THAT DAY. 'You've had to listen to two confessions today. You clearly have a talent for it, ever thought about being a priest?'

'No thank you.'

'So we know now that Sir Graywood was regularly smuggling cargo into West India Docks,' said Philip. 'He was paying off PC Buller and PC Milton and it wouldn't surprise me if he was paying off a few other people too.'

'Sergeant Finch?'

'It's possible, isn't it? Perhaps the entire Port of London Authority police force agreed to turn a blind eye. Maybe that's unfair of me, but it makes you wonder, doesn't it? I spoke to Detective Inspector Jenkins about Rupert Graywood's kidnap and he's organising a team of men to be at Hyde Park tomorrow.'

'Excellent, thank you Philip.'

'He also told me they've just found evidence in Sir Graywood's secret room that Captain Pegwell was complicit in the smuggling operation.'

'He knew about it?'

'It seems so. Jenkins is planning to interview Pegwell about it. There's probably no need for us to be surprised, is there? But Pegwell's a good liar, that's for sure.'

'What's the actual evidence?'

'Telegrams apparently. Jenkins says he found a lot of communication with the cocaine factory in Germany and some of that was sent and received by Pegwell.'

'But he didn't know about the secret room?'

'No. It appears not.'

'So it's possible Graywood and Pegwell fell out over the smuggling,' said Augusta. 'And Pegwell knew Graywood would be at the dock that night, so he went there, murdered him and escaped in his van.'

'That's a likely possibility.'

'I wonder if Captain Pegwell had an affair with Miss Claydene?' said Augusta.

'What makes you say that?'

'If the two men had been rivals for Miss Claydene's affections, then that would strengthen the motive for Pegwell murdering Graywood.'

'I agree.'

'We just need Captain Pegwell or Miss Claydene to confirm or deny it,' said Augusta.

'Well you seem to be very good at getting confessions out of people, Augusta. Why don't you ask them?'

'Perhaps I will. But first of all, I need to help Aunt Lydia with the ransom demand. It's important we get Rupert back safely tomorrow morning.'

Chapter 39

THE STATUE OF ACHILLES IN HYDE PARK STOOD AT THE southeastern end of the park, near Hyde Park Corner. It was only half a mile from Aunt Lydia's home, but she insisted on her chauffeur driving her and Augusta there in the shiny blue Napier limousine.

'What's the time?' she asked Augusta.

'Half-past nine.'

'Oh, half an hour yet. I'm so nervous!'

'Why don't we walk in the park for a bit?'

It was a beautiful early autumn morning.

'Very well.'

They got out of the car, and the chauffeur collected the bag of money from the boot. Scotland Yard had delivered it to Aunt Lydia's home the previous evening, hidden in a box of fruit and vegetables from the grocer.

They took the path which ran alongside Rotten Row. The park stretched wide under a blue sky, its green lawns glowing in the golden sunshine. Leaves floated gently from the autumnal trees. It was a mild day with no breeze at all.

Despite the mild temperature, Aunt Lydia wore a long turquoise overcoat and a fur stole.

'I wonder where Rupert is now?' said Aunt Lydia, clinging to Augusta's arm. 'I've been so worried about him! Do you think the kidnapper will bring him with him? Or will he go back to wherever he's been holding him and release him then?'

'I'm not sure,' said Augusta. 'We need to wait for the police to arrest him.'

'But if he sees them, then he won't pick up the money, will he?'

'They'll all be in plain clothes and acting like normal people enjoying the park today. See that gentleman over there? He could be an undercover police officer and you wouldn't know it.'

'So all I need to do is walk up to the statue and leave the bag there as he asked me to do. And then I get away again as quickly as possible. I don't want him to discover there's no real money in the bag. I hope I'm out of sight before he does.'

'I'm sure you will be,' said Augusta. 'And the police will be ready to seize him, too. I realise this feels rather daunting, but with the police present, I hope we don't have much to worry about.'

'It's very difficult to put your trust in them, isn't it? Anyway, all I should do is follow the orders. And that's all I can do, isn't it?'

'Yes, Aunt Lydia.'

'I want to thank you, Augusta, for being such an enormous help to me during this time. I want to apologise for how rude I was to you during our first few meetings. I suppose I still thought of you as that young woman who'd walked out on her family and I resented you for that. And now I can see what an interesting life you've made for yourself.'

Augusta calmed herself with a breath before she asked her next question. 'Have you told my father yet about me?' she asked.

'Not yet. The truth is... we fell out a few years ago. He sent me a telegram expressing his sympathies when Frederick died. But he hasn't called on me and I haven't called on him. But I feel now I would like to so I can tell him what a fine young woman you are.'

Augusta laughed. 'But that's not an accurate description. I'm not young, I'm forty.'

'You don't look it.'

'And as for fine.'

'I think you're a very interesting person, Augusta. And you still haven't told me what you did for British intelligence during the war. I want to find out, you know.'

'I shall tell you one day, Aunt Lydia,' said Augusta. 'But not now. We need to concentrate on getting Rupert back safe.'

'Yes, we do. What's the time?'

'We have ten minutes to go.'

'Oh goodness! Let's turn around then and start heading for the statue. But as we get close, Augusta, you'll need to leave me. He told me to go to the statue on my own. We don't want to do anything which might anger him.'

'I agree,' said Augusta. 'I'll wait for you out of sight.'

As they drew nearer to the statue of Achilles, Augusta stopped and watched Aunt Lydia continue along the path with the bag in her hand. She had a slight limp and seemed vulnerable.

Augusta prayed the Yard would keep her safe.

Once her aunt had disappeared from view, Augusta checked her watch. It was almost ten o'clock.

A nanny walked past, pushing a perambulator. Birds sang in the trees.

Everything was calm and peaceful. A church clock somewhere near the park struck ten. Augusta watched and waited. Her shoulders were tense and her breathing felt short and shallow.

Then movement caught her eye, and she saw the unmistakable turquoise overcoat of Aunt Lydia. She was walking as fast as she could towards Augusta and attempted to jog from time to time. She no longer had the bag in her hand.

Augusta walked towards her. 'I did it,' said Aunt Lydia, panting. 'I didn't see him. I just left it by the statue and left as soon as I heard a clock strike ten.'

Augusta led her to a nearby bench and urged her to sit down and rest. 'I don't think I should,' said Aunt Lydia. 'What if he comes after me?'

'The police will get him first,' said Augusta. 'I feel sure of it.'

'But where is he? I didn't see him. I didn't see the police either. I just left the bag by the statue. What if someone else finds it and picks it up?'

'Well, there's nothing valuable in there for them.'

'But if they take it away, then the kidnapper might think I haven't turned up after all. He might harm Rupert!'

They were interrupted by a shout which carried across the park.

'Goodness,' said Aunt Lydia. 'Is that them?'

'Yes, it could be,' said Augusta. 'I should think it's safe now to get a little nearer.'

'Nearer? No, thank you! I want to leave.'

Augusta was keen to see what was happening with the police and the kidnapper.

'Don't you want to see them arrest him?'

'Well, I suppose so,' said Aunt Lydia. Augusta could understand why she was worried.

'Come along,' said Augusta, taking her arm. 'I'm sure we can get a little nearer now. They must have got him.'

More shouting followed, and Augusta and Aunt Lydia neared the statue. As they got closer, they could see a bundle of dark-clothed men huddling on the ground.

The lean figure of a man she recognised as Detective Inspector Jenkins stood over them. Augusta smiled. 'We're safe. They have him. Now they can get Rupert.'

'Oh, thank goodness!'

Detective Inspector Jenkins noticed them and beckoned them over. The bag which Lady Graywood had dropped off lay close by.

'He can't cause any more trouble now,' he said.

Two plainclothes police officers hauled a young man to his feet. He was in his early twenties and was thin and feeble looking.

'You're sure he's the kidnapper?' said Augusta.

'Quite sure,' said Detective Inspector Jenkins. 'He was clearly watching the drop-off point from the bushes over there. As soon as Lady Graywood left, he emerged and ran over to pick up the bag. It's our chap all right.' He turned to the young man, who had bits of grass on his suit. 'What's your name?'

'Andrew Stanley-Sullivan,' he stammered. He was well spoken.

'Well, I think you know why you're under arrest, Sullivan.'

'Stanley-Sullivan.'

'Where's Rupert?' asked Lady Graywood.

'At the house,' muttered the youth.

'Which house?' asked Jenkins.

'Twenty-three Albemarle Street, Mayfair.'

'Close by, then,' said Jenkins. He ordered two men to go to the address and told the others to take the young man into custody.

'Thank you, Detective,' said Lady Graywood. 'This is such a relief.'

'We need to make sure your stepson is all right, Lady Graywood.'

'Absolutely.'

'We'll get everyone over to the park police station, Lady Graywood. We'll bring Rupert there too once my men have fetched him. If he needs medical treatment, they'll summon a doctor. We shall see you there.'

Chapter 40

Aunt Lydia's chauffeur drove them to the Hyde Park police station in the centre of the park. It was a red brick building with large sash windows, a row of dormer windows in the roof and a balustraded porch. It was so pleasing to the eye that it looked like a country house to Augusta.

Once they were inside, they were shown to a wood-panelled waiting room.

'Why won't they let me see Rupert?' asked Aunt Lydia.

'They may not have brought him to the station yet,' said Augusta. 'Do you recognise the young man they've arrested?'

'No. I've no idea who he is. How did he even manage to kidnap Rupert? He seems so young and rather skinny, too. I'm surprised he was able to physically overpower him.'

'Maybe he threatened him with a weapon.'

'Oh yes, I hadn't thought of that. I suppose so. Poor Rupert! He must have been through quite an ordeal. I suppose the young man was just an opportunist. He'd read about Frederick's death and committed this despicable act on our family. Rupert and I haven't seen eye to eye over the years, but this episode has helped me realise that I feel some fondness for him. I've been extremely worried about him and I wouldn't wish this ordeal on anyone.'

Detective Inspector Jenkins joined them. 'How are you, Lady Graywood?'

'As well as can be, Detective. Well done for apprehending the kidnapper. What's his story?'

'Well, it's an interesting story. He's told us a rather strange tale, which I'm going to have to corroborate with your stepson when he arrives here.'

'What is this strange tale?'

'I think it's best if you hear it from the horse's mouth. Come with me and speak to Mr Stanley-Sullivan yourself. He'll tell you what he's told me. And when Mr Graywood arrives, we can find out if it's the truth.'

They followed Jenkins to a drab room with grey walls. Two constables stood guard. Andrew Stanley-Sullivan looked dishevelled. He had a grass stain on his cheek and he sat at a table with his wrists in handcuffs.

'This is Lady Graywood,' Detective Inspector Jenkins told him. 'The recently widowed lady who you menaced over the telephone. I expect you feel rather sorry for yourself now, don't you?'

The young man gave a sulky nod.

'Now perhaps you can tell Lady Graywood what you've just told me.'

The young man looked down at the table. Then he shuffled in his chair and the chains of his handcuffs clinked.

'It was all Rupert's idea,' he said.

'Rupert's idea?' said Aunt Lydia. 'What a load of

nonsense! My stepson can't be at fault for his own kidnapping.'

'I think you'd better explain a bit more, Stanley-Sullivan,' said Jenkins.

He cleared his throat. 'I didn't kidnap Rupert. He just wanted me to pretend that I had. He wanted the money.'

Aunt Lydia gasped, and Augusta grabbed her arm to steady her. A constable pulled over a chair so she could sit in it.

'Are you saying Rupert pretended to be kidnapped?' she asked.

Mr Stanley-Sullivan nodded. 'I told him it was a silly idea, but he was insistent about going through with it. And then when he said we could split the money, I agreed.'

'Even though it wasn't a very generous split,' said Jenkins. 'I believe he said you could have a quarter, didn't he?'

'Yes. Two and a half thousand pounds. It's still a lot of money to me and that's why I said yes.'

'Well, what a foolish young man you are!' said Aunt Lydia. 'You clearly had no thought about how upsetting it was for me to receive your nasty telephone calls. I've just been widowed, and you thought it was fun to telephone me and threaten me! Do you realise I've barely slept for two nights and two days?'

'I'm sorry,' he muttered. 'I only did what Rupert told me to do.'

'Quite astonishing,' said Aunt Lydia. 'Am I really to believe that my stepson pretended he was kidnapped so he could extort ten thousand pounds from me? His widowed stepmother?'

'That's what Mr Stanley-Sullivan is saying,' said Jenkins. 'But let's see what Mr Graywood says.'

They didn't have long to wait. A knock at the door preceded the entry of two plain clothed police officers and

Rupert Graywood. He wore a striped silk housecoat of red and lilac and had the expression of a naughty schoolboy who'd just been caught out.

'Rupert Graywood,' said Aunt Lydia. 'Am I to believe what this young man is telling me? You set up this whole kidnap business?'

'It was a silly idea, Stepmother,' he said.

'So it's true? You're not even going to deny it?'

'I don't know what else to say. I didn't think it would end up like this.'

'You put me through a hellish few days, just so you could try to get your hands on ten thousand pounds of my money?'

'My father's money.'

'Your father didn't leave any money. He only left debts!'

Rupert said nothing.

'You've both committed an extremely serious offence,' said Jenkins. 'Poor Lady Graywood has been through a torrid time, and the pair of you inflicted this dreadful scheme on her. Have you no shame? Have you no respect? It's appalling behaviour. And entirely unsuccessful. It wasn't very well thought through, was it? You foolishly thought Lady Graywood would be too frightened to inform the police. But you were wrong. She's shown great bravery indeed.'

Aunt Lydia pulled out a handkerchief and wiped her eyes. Augusta felt sorry for her. She'd been very worried about Rupert and all the time he'd been deceiving her.

'I'm sorry,' said Rupert. 'That's all I can say. I have debts too. They need to be paid off, and I suppose this was a desperate measure. I didn't realise Father had left nothing.'

'Your friend here even suggested I should sell my house!' said Aunt Lydia. 'You were willing to make me homeless? And to think I was worried about you. You're a despicable piece of work, Rupert Graywood. I was polite to you when your father was alive because I considered it my duty to do so. But after this, you've completely lost my loyalty. I shall do whatever I can to ensure that you inherit nothing.'

She got to her feet.

'You're an ungrateful young man,' she continued. 'I brought you up as my own son, even though I never liked you very much. I did everything you and your father required of me. And this is how you repay me? I really can't bear to be in your presence a moment longer.'

She left the room.

Chapter 41

Augusta accompanied Aunt Lydia home.

'I suppose I shouldn't be surprised,' she said as the chauffeur steered the car out of Hyde Park. 'I never did like Rupert very much. It sounds awful to say it because I'm all he has now his father has died. And I tried with him, I really did. And I genuinely felt worried for him, too. I really feared he would be harmed. What a waste of my time! He cares for no one but himself. It doesn't matter to him that I'm already grieving over the death of his father. You'd think he would have had some sympathy, because he's grieving too.'

'Maybe his grief is the reason he behaved erratically,' said Augusta.

'No, it wasn't erratic behaviour. It's actually quite normal for Rupert. I should have seen through it! He doesn't care a jot about me. All he wants is the money. And isn't it amusing that there's no money for him? I've been left with nothing but debt. And I shall alter my will to ensure that, after my death, the proceeds from the sale of the house and its contents will go to my children and not Rupert. He won't inherit a thing.'

'The police will punish him and his friend for their actions,' said Augusta.

'Good. But I don't want him to become too much of a distraction for Jenkins. He needs to work on finding my husband's murderer! I'm really struggling to remain patient.'

'What a horrible young man,' said Philip when Augusta told him Rupert had faked his own kidnap. 'Fancy doing such a thing to his grieving stepmother. Jenkins will make sure he's suitably punished, I'm certain of it.'

'It was extremely heartless of Rupert,' said Augusta. 'He's clearly desperate to get his hands on some money. He mentioned he had debts of his own.'

'I wonder how?' said Philip. 'Gambling, or perhaps some other vice.'

'If Rupert really is desperate and cruel, you wonder what lengths he would go to in order to get his hands on money,' said Augusta.

'His father's murder?'

'It's a possibility, isn't it? Perhaps he assumed his father had left him something in his will.'

'So you're suggesting he could have murdered his own father in the hope he would inherit some of his father's money? When that wasn't forthcoming, he tried to blackmail his stepmother for it. It's a possibility, isn't it? That idea may already have occurred to Jenkins. Hopefully, he's asking Rupert if he has an alibi for the night of his father's death.'

Chapter 42

'YOU AND STANLEY-SULLIVAN THOUGHT YOU WERE VERY clever,' Detective Inspector Jenkins said to Rupert Graywood. 'But you weren't, were you? You were stupid.'

'Can I have a break now?' asked Rupert. He'd been stuck in the little grey room with the detective for almost an hour. Rupert had told him the fake kidnap had been Andrew's idea. And it was Andrew's fault it had gone wrong, too. Andrew had taken advantage of a grieving friend while he was at his lowest point.

He felt sure the detective believed him.

'We'll have a break shortly,' said Jenkins. 'But before then, I want to ask you about your father.'

Rupert gave a sniff. 'But you know how upsetting it will be for me!'

Jenkins opened a file which a constable had brought into him five minutes earlier. 'I've just had this fetched from Scotland Yard,' he said. 'And in here are the notes from an interview you had with Detective Inspector Morris.'

'I don't recall it. Everything since my father's death has been a blur.'

'How did you get on with your father?' asked Jenkins.

'Fine.'

'Just fine?'

'We were very different. I'm like my mother, but she died when I was twelve, so it was just me and my father until Lady Buchanan came along.'

'She's now Lady Graywood?'

'Yes. My stepmother.'

'I think we know how you feel about her.'

'Yes, and it caused ructions with my father. I was never the son he wanted me to be. But eventually he found a use for me in his company. There was a time when I hoped I would succeed him, but he didn't think I was up to it. And then I made a slight mistake a few weeks ago, and he moved me to the billing office.'

'That angered you?'

'Yes. There was no need for it.'

Jenkins read through the papers in front of him. 'It says here you were in the Midnight Lounge in Soho on the night of your father's death.'

'Yes. I had a few drinks with friends and I had no idea my father was at the docks that night.'

'But you left early, didn't you? Witnesses say they saw you leave around midnight.'

Rupert's jaw tightened. He swallowed hard, trying to stay calm.

'I… stepped out for some air. You know how it is.'

'You were seen getting into a taxi.'

'Yes. I went home.'

'It says here your valet heard you return home about four o'clock.'

Rupert sighed. Matheson was always frustratingly honest. Couldn't he at least lie for once?

He pulled the cigarette packet out of his pocket. It was empty.

'Fine,' he said. 'I'll tell you everything that happened if you can give me a cigarette.'

'Sounds like a straightforward deal,' said the detective, taking a packet out of his jacket pocket.

Once Rupert had lit his cigarette, he leant back and stared up at the ceiling.

'The plan was I would meet the van at a Chinese laundry in Limehouse at half-past three.'

'Which van?'

'My father's van.'

'Your father was driving it?'

'Yes. But it didn't turn up.'

'He planned to drive the van from West India Dock?'

'Yes.'

'It had something in it?'

'Well, obviously, yes. The cargo from Antwerp.'

'Cocaine?'

'I believe so.'

'You knew your father was smuggling drugs?' Jenkins sat back in his chair and folded his arms.

Rupert didn't want to admit it directly. He took a long inhale on his cigarette. 'He asked me to help him,' he said eventually. 'He was very insistent about it. I couldn't turn him down.'

'Was it the first time you helped him?'

'Not really, no.'

'You regularly helped him?'

'Yes, I did. But I don't want to get into trouble for this. He was the one doing all the smuggling. I just did what I was told.'

'So what was your role?'

'I liaised with the customers.'

'And on that night, the customer was a Chinese laundry?'

'Yes. But I think you know what I mean by that.'

'I know exactly what you mean. The gangster Mr Yu owned several laundries and restaurants in the Limehouse and Poplar area and used them to distribute opium and cocaine. He's currently serving a long sentence in Wandsworth prison for his crimes, but despite that, we know his empire endures. Did the laundry you go to belong to Mr Yu?'

'I don't know. I only know the nice lady who runs it. Mrs Lee.'

Jenkins made some notes. 'We shall have a word with her. Not only because she might have some connection to Mr Yu, but also because she could provide you with a useful alibi for that night.'

Rupert warmed to this idea. 'Oh yes, she can. She'll tell you I was there. We drank jasmine tea together while we waited.'

'Well, let's hope she can help you out, because it doesn't look very good for you at the moment, does it? You were angry at your father because he didn't give you an important role in his company. And you knew he was going to be in West India Dock that night to collect the shipment of cocaine from the *Colonia*.'

'I didn't murder him!'

'We'll know soon enough who it was. And if it wasn't you, Mr Graywood, then who was it?'

Rupert gritted his teeth. 'Pegwell.'

Chapter 43

'You'll be alright locking up will you, Polly?' said Nancy Claydene as she reapplied her lipstick.

'Yes I will, Miss Claydene.'

'I'll see you tomorrow then.'

'I'm not in tomorrow, Miss Claydene.'

'Not in?'

'You let me have a day's holiday so I could see my brother off.'

'Oh, that's right. He's going to America, isn't he?' Nancy turned back to the mirror and adjusted her fuchsia pink hat. 'I remember now.' She'd forgotten. And now she was going to be in the shop on her own all day tomorrow. Unless she could move a girl from one of the other shops. But she was short of staff ever since Miss Hindson's sudden departure from the Tottenham Court Road store.

'Bon voyage to your brother, Polly!' She looped her handbag over her arm and headed for the door.

'Thank you, Miss Claydene!'

Outside on Bond Street, she looked about for a cab.

'Hello Nancy,' came a voice from behind her. She spun round.

'Thomas Pegwell! You startled me.'

He chuckled. 'How's your day been?'

'Alright.' He looked her up and down, and she pouted a little. She found Captain Pegwell quite attractive in a rugged, seafaring sort of way. 'How's your day been?' she asked.

'It's all the better for seeing you here, Nancy.'

'Oh, here we go.' She gave a coy smile. 'Are you here to proposition me again?'

'I thought with old Graywood out of the way, I'd try my luck again,' he said.

'Oh Thomas! You're not supposed to know about that.'

She strolled towards Oxford Street and he fell into step with her. She hoped she wouldn't have to walk too far because her shoes were pinching her feet.

'So where are you off to now?' he asked.

'To see Lydia. I'm trying to find a cab.'

'Perhaps you have time for a drink with me first?'

'I can't, Thomas. It's only been twelve days since Frederick died. It's disrespectful to his memory.'

'Oh, come on, Nancy. If you were his widow, then I'd be respectful about it. But you were his mistress and—'

She stopped and turned to him, offended. 'And that means I'm not as important?'

'You're very important, Nancy. I've told you that enough times, haven't I? But no one's expecting you to be in mourning, so it doesn't matter if you take up with a handsome captain, does it?'

'It would matter to your wife.' She continued walking.

'She's about to divorce me,' he said, keeping up with her.

Nancy laughed. 'I've heard that one before! Practically every man I meet tells me his wife is about to divorce him.'

'It's the effect you have on men, Nancy.'

'Is that so?' She grinned.

A tall, lean man stepped in front of them. Nancy gasped.

'Captain Pegwell,' he said.

'Not you again!' said Thomas.

Nancy stared at the scowling, lean man. 'Who are you?' she asked. But he ignored her and showed Thomas his warrant card.

'You're coming with us.'

Nancy gasped.

'No, I'm not!' said Thomas. 'Get lost, Jenkins, before I... ouch!' Two constables grabbed his arms. 'Get off me!' he cried.

People stared. A police van pulled up next to the pavement.

Nancy backed away. She didn't want to be part of it.

'Nancy!' Thomas called out to her. 'Tell them to let me go! I'm an innocent man!'

She shook her head and trotted away. Glancing back over her shoulder, she saw Thomas being pushed into the van.

What was he being arrested for? Murder?

She gave a little cry of dismay and held her hand out for a taxi.

Chapter 44

'GOOD MORNING, AUGUSTA!' DR WILLIAM LENNOX strode into the shop with a bunch of colourful carnations in his hand. 'For you,' he said, handing them to her.

The gesture felt too much for her. She was tired from the previous day and didn't feel particularly jovial.

'Thank you, William.' She rested the flowers on the counter and forced a smile.

Fred slipped away through the door to the workshop.

'How are you, Augusta?' Dr Lennox's smile was charming and there was little doubt he was a handsome man. Augusta worried she'd been rather harsh to judge him for his loud laugh.

'I'm alright,' she said. 'Just a little bit tired. It's been a busy few days.'

'You do so much, Augusta. You're a private detective and you run this shop. It would tire me out, too. How are you getting on with your investigation?'

'Well, it was complicated by Rupert Graywood, who pretended to my aunt that he'd been kidnapped. He asked his friend to demand a ransom from her.'

'Did he? What a dreadful fellow! And you had to deal with that, did you?'

'I helped my aunt. She was very distressed.'

'I can imagine. Just awful. There are some strange people about. As evidenced by these nasty letters I keep receiving. I've got another one to take to Mr Fisher in a moment.'

'And you still have no idea who's writing them?'

'None. Mr Fisher will get to the bottom of it. I know he will. I won't detain you much longer but just quickly... I want to tell you how much I enjoyed our dinner the other evening. You're delightful company, Augusta, and I would feel most honoured if you would join me for dinner again another time.' He scratched his chin and Augusta smiled at his awkwardness. 'It doesn't have to be soon,' he continued. 'Just whenever you feel like it. If you feel like it, that is. Perhaps you don't. And that would be fine. I would respect your decision either way, but I—'

'Yes, I would like to,' she said.

'You would?' He seemed surprised. 'Well, thank you.' He grinned. 'Thank you very much indeed, Augusta. When would be a good time?'

'Next Tuesday?'

'Tuesday. Yes, that would be wonderful. Now I hope you're not agreeing to this so as not to offend me. If you don't want to go to dinner then—'

'No, it's fine. I do.'

'Excellent.'

Augusta heard footsteps on the stairs and Philip appeared. 'Oh, I'm sorry,' he said as soon as he saw Dr Lennox. 'I'll go back up.'

'No, Mr Fisher, please don't!' said William. 'I was just about to come and see you.'

'Were you?'

Philip walked over to the counter, leaning on his walking stick for support. 'Flowers?' he said. 'How lovely.'

'They're for Augusta,' said William.

'Oh. I thought you'd bought them for me,' said Philip.

Dr Lennox gave a loud laugh. 'You're an amusing man, Fisher. Here, I've received another letter this morning.' He pulled it out of his jacket pocket and handed it to Philip.

'Another one.' He sighed. 'I think I've narrowed it down to three possible suspects now.'

'Have you? Who?' asked Dr Lennox.

'Mr Trendle, Miss King and Colonel Scott.'

'Interesting. I wouldn't be surprised if it's Colonel Scott. But Miss King does surprise me.'

'Why don't we discuss it a little more in my office?'

'Of course. We don't want to be using Augusta's shop for business, do we?' Dr Lennox chuckled.

Philip turned to Augusta. 'I came down to let you know Jenkins arrested Captain Pegwell yesterday.'

'Brilliant news!'

'And Rupert's confessed to helping his father with the smuggling.'

'He was involved too? Goodness, Detective Inspector Jenkins is doing a good job.'

'Yes, he's got Pegwell and Rupert in custody,' said Philip. 'Not without your help, Augusta. But anyway, he seems slightly grateful for it now and says he'll keep me updated.'

'Thank you Philip.'

'Shall we discuss the latest letter, Dr Lennox?' said Philip.

'Yes indeed.' William turned to Augusta. 'Cheerio, Augusta. I'm off to Fisher's office now. But I shall telephone you about next Tuesday.'

Philip gave her a quick sidelong glance and Augusta wished William hadn't mentioned it in front of him.

The rest of the day felt oddly quiet. With Captain Pegwell and Rupert Graywood in custody, Augusta wasn't sure if it was worth her while trying to do more on the case. If one of them confessed to being the murderer, then her work was done.

It seemed a shame for everything to end quite so abruptly and quietly.

She showed Fred how to stitch sections of pages together and he attempted it with his fingers fumbling over the needle and thread.

'Oh dear, I'm no good at this,' he said.

'You just need practice.'

'My fingers are too fat.'

'They're not! They're normal sized.'

'They're fatter than your fingers and I can't grip the needle properly.'

'You'll manage it, Fred. Perhaps your mother has some needlework you can practise with at home?'

'Yes, she probably does. But if I'm this bad at it, then she won't let me! Ouch!'

'Have you pricked your finger again?'

Fred nodded as he sucked on his forefinger. 'I think I'll just do the easy books for now,' he said.

Augusta took over the stitching while Fred cleaned a book cover.

'I keep wondering if there's something I've missed,' she said as she worked.

'About what?'

'Oh sorry, Fred. I'm just thinking aloud. Sir Graywood's murder. I feel like there's something I've missed. I keep going over the detail of what happened that evening and yet... that's it. What happened to the van?'

'What van?'

'The van loaded with the cases of cocaine from the ship. Sir Graywood's murderer must have driven it away. He could have taken the van because he wanted to steal the drugs. Or he took the van because it was an easy vehicle to get away in. So it could have been another smuggler or a gangster. Or even Captain Pegwell. Maybe Rupert Graywood? Or even Nancy Claydene?'

'And you're wondering where the van is now?' asked Fred.

'Yes. And the cases of cocaine which were in it. Detective Inspector Morris thinks the drugs could have been worth two thousand pounds. Where have the van and the cocaine gone?'

'Someone's hidden the van and sold the cocaine.'

'The cocaine would probably be fairly easy to sell. But only if you have someone you can sell it to. As for the van, that's not easy to hide.'

'I'm sure the police will find it,' said Fred.

'Yes, they probably will,' said Augusta.

It seemed a shame to leave everything to the police now.

Chapter 45

THAT EVENING, AUGUSTA DECIDED TO FORGET ALL ABOUT the investigation. She made herself a cup of cocoa, picked up a book of poems by Elizabeth Barrett Browning and put a blanket over her lap.

Sparky fluttered from the curtain rail to the lampshade and back. Then he perched on the back of the sofa, as if reading the book of poems over her shoulder.

'You understand every word, don't you, Sparky?' said Augusta.

The evening wore on and her eyelids grew heavy. When the knock sounded at the door, she couldn't decide whether or not she'd been asleep.

She peered through the peephole in the door and saw Philip standing there. Immediately she worried.

'Is everything alright?' she asked as soon as she opened the door.

'Yes. Just about.'

'Just about? Come in.'

Philip took off his hat as he stepped inside. 'Hello Sparky,' he said. 'Isn't it past your bedtime, little fellow?'

187

'Oh yes, I need to put him back in his cage,' said Augusta. 'I forgot the time. I think I fell asleep.'

'I'm sorry,' said Philip. 'You're tired. I should leave. I can speak to you tomorrow.'

'Leave? You've just climbed all those stairs. Sit down and I'll make you a drink. What would you like?'

'What are you having?'

'Cocoa, but it's gone cold.'

'Erm, cold cocoa then please.'

'I'll pour us both a whisky.'

Augusta handed Philip his drink, then sat down, smoothing her hair to improve her appearance.

'So is everything alright?' she asked. Philip didn't call on her very often, especially late in the evening.

'Yes. Sort of.' He sat up stiffly. 'I worked late today and thought I'd call on you before I go home. I suppose there's something I want to say about... erm, this Lennox chap.'

'Yes?'

'I've been looking through all the unpleasant letters he's been sent and he's obviously upset someone.'

'Do you know why?'

'I think I know why. But really...' He rubbed his brow. 'Oh, it's not my place to say it. In fact, I shouldn't have come here. You're very fond of him, Augusta, and he's very fond of you, so really it has nothing to do with me.'

Augusta cradled her glass in her hand and watched him. 'You're not making much sense, Philip.'

'Am I not? Oh dear. I don't know why I find these things so difficult.' He took a gulp of whisky. 'In short then. Don't go to dinner with him again.'

'I'm sorry? Are you telling me what to do?'

'Not really. Perhaps that came out wrong. It was supposed to be more of a suggestion.'

'It didn't sound like a suggestion. It sounded like an order.'

'Did it?' He rubbed his brow again. 'I knew I shouldn't have come here. I should have just gone straight home. It's just that... I was reading those letters and then I remembered the flowers he bought you. Oh, and there they are, in fact.' He pointed to them in the vase on the dining table. 'They look very pretty.'

'Why don't you want me to go to dinner again with Dr Lennox?' Augusta asked.

'Because I don't think he's very nice. He's a charming, handsome, war hero. But I think there's another side to him.'

Augusta felt a ball of anger grow in her stomach. 'You can't decide for me who I choose to go to dinner with, Philip. It's completely unreasonable! I can go to dinner with whomever I want. And maybe there is another side to him. No one's perfect. There's another side to you as well.'

'Is there?'

'Yes.'

'What other side?'

'A grumpy side. And I've thought of another one, too. A secretive side.'

'Secretive?'

'Yes. You didn't tell me anything about your time by the coast with your wife.'

'There was nothing to tell.'

'But there must have been. You were away for two weeks!'

Philip got to his feet. 'I wanted to spend time with my son, Augusta. I only see him every few weeks.'

'And your wife? She telephoned you when I was in your office last week and I had to leave. It was the only reason I said yes to Dr Lennox's dinner invitation.'

'What? I don't understand.'

Augusta stood up to face him. 'Dr Lennox invited me out to dinner shortly after your wife telephoned you.'

'My estranged wife, Augusta.'

'But I assumed you'd reconciled.'

'Why?' Philip looked baffled.

'Because you seemed well when you returned, and you didn't tell me anything about your time away, and then she telephoned you.'

'To remind me it was the dog's birthday.'

'The dog's birthday?'

'Yes! I always forget. I'm hopeless at remembering birthdays.'

'But the dog's birthday? Herbert the dachshund?'

'Yes, that's right. My estranged wife puts a lot of importance on these things.'

'I see. So you're not reconciled?'

'No! She was unfaithful to me with my friend, Augusta. And although she's the mother of my child, I can't forgive her for that. Or my friend for that matter. The pair of them are as bad as each other.'

'I see. I'm sorry. I thought…' Augusta's felt her shoulders sink at the misunderstanding.

'You thought wrong. And what a mistake it was because it meant you then agreed to dinner with Doctor Charming and now he's bought you flowers and you're going out for a second time. And when I dare mention it, you accuse me of telling you what to do.'

'Because you did! You told me not to go to dinner with him!'

'It came out all wrong, Augusta. I didn't mean it like that. Oh… can't you see it?' His eyes held hers. 'Can't you see why I said it all wrong like that? I'm hopeless at these things, I really am. I don't want you to go to dinner with

Dr Lennox again because I care about you so much, Augusta. Too much in fact. Perhaps it's even... oh, I don't know.' He rubbed at his face and Augusta stared at him, struggling to believe what he was telling her.

'You care?' she said.

'Yes! I thought you knew!'

'How?'

'I don't know! Perhaps I played things down a bit because we work together and I didn't want to make anything too obvious.'

Augusta looked down at the floor. She felt dazed and light-headed. 'It wasn't obvious at all,' she said. 'It was completely unobvious, in fact. I'd hoped that maybe... But then there's your wife...'

'Estranged wife. Forget about her.'

She met his gaze again. 'Alright then. I'm happy to do that.'

They both took a step towards each other.

'Really?' said Philip.

'Yes. I can forget about your estranged wife.'

'But can you forget about Dr Lennox?'

'Who?'

Philip laughed. 'Oh, Augusta. This is why I'm so fond of you.'

He leant in and their lips met.

It was a moment Augusta had imagined but never thought possible. She felt weak with happiness. He put his warm arms around her and steadied her.

She pulled away for a moment. 'What did you get Herbert for his birthday?'

'A ball. An extra tough one which he can't destroy within five minutes. I posted it a few days ago.'

'I'm sure he'll love it.'

'He will.'

They were about to kiss again but the telephone rang.

'Oh,' said Augusta. She released herself from the embrace, feeling a little embarrassed and also stunned by the telephone's interruption. 'I should answer that.'

'Yes.'

'Hello?' she said into the receiver.

'Augusta? It's Aunt Lydia. You won't believe what's happened. Nancy's been murdered!'

Chapter 46

'MY FRIEND! OH, MY DEAR, DEAR FRIEND!' SAID AUNT Lydia.

Augusta sat next to her on the settee in the drawing room. Her aunt wouldn't have been so upset if she'd known Nancy had been having an affair with her husband. Augusta wondered if it would ever be appropriate to tell her. It was something she was going to keep secret for the time being.

Lottie brought in tea, even though it was half-past ten in the evening. She clearly thought it could be a comfort to Lady Graywood. The lean black cat watched them from a chair.

'I don't understand,' said Aunt Lydia. 'It's just one thing after another! First Frederick and now Nancy.' She turned to Augusta. 'Is someone trying to punish me? Why are they taking everyone away from me?'

'It must be awful for you, Aunt Lydia. What happened to Nancy?'

'She was in her shop. Apparently, she was on her own

today because her usual girl, Polly, had the day off. She was found in the room at the back.'

Augusta recalled the comfortable little room with its velvet chairs and fabric-draped walls.

'It was a passer-by who alerted the police,' said Aunt Lydia. 'The shop was still open long after the surrounding ones had closed. The lights were still on and the door was unlocked. He went inside to inform the owner and there was no sign of anyone. Someone could have gone in there and taken something and raided the till! But luckily they didn't. The poor chap found Nancy in the room at the back. She was lying face down on the floor. Oh, it must have been horrible!'

'Do they know how she died?' asked Augusta.

'She was hit over the head with something heavy. The intruder must have caught her by surprise. Maybe it was Rupert? He's angry at me because his kidnap plan failed. And so he's decided to murder my friend. It's his revenge, isn't it?'

'He couldn't have attacked Miss Claydene,' said Augusta. 'He's in police custody.'

'So he is!' Her eyes grew wide. 'So who did this, do you think?'

'Not Captain Pegwell, because he's in custody, too.'

'Then it's a mystery.' She dabbed at her eyes with her handkerchief. 'Perhaps it's one of those smugglers,' she said.

'What do you mean?'

'Detective Inspector Jenkins called on me yesterday after he'd finished questioning Rupert. He told me all about Frederick's involvement with drug smuggling and how Rupert and Pegwell knew about it, too. It sickens me, it really does! Frederick was caught up in something very dangerous. Detective Inspector Jenkins thinks another smuggler murdered Frederick and stole his van that night. And Nancy Claydene must have been caught up in it too! I really don't know how.'

Augusta wondered if she should mention the affair. But then she thought better of it.

'So maybe Nancy knew something?' said Aunt Lydia. 'Perhaps she knew who murdered Frederick? If she did, then I really wish she could have told the police. Then they would have got him and she wouldn't be dead!'

'Perhaps she was too scared to tell them?'

'She probably was. But she needed to be brave and sadly she wasn't!'

Fresh tears sprung into her eyes and she wiped them away. 'I want a policeman guarding my door at night,' she said. 'I don't feel safe. Will you speak to the police about it, Augusta? My husband's been murdered and so has my friend. I'm worried I'll be next! Nobody knows what it's like for me at the moment. Just a few weeks ago, my life was normal. And now look at it! It's complete chaos and I'm caught in the middle of it. I feel like I'm a ship being tossed around on a stormy sea. And there's no safe harbour, Augusta. I'm in danger of capsizing, I know it!'

Augusta poured her another cup of tea and put plenty of sugar in it. 'What did Sir Graywood's van look like?' she asked.

'Van? What van?'

'The van he drove to the docks to collect the cases of cocaine,' said Augusta. 'Do you know what it looked like?'

'No. I never saw it. And I didn't know about it until the police told me about it. I suppose Frederick must have kept it in the docks somewhere.'

'The murderer escaped in it,' said Augusta. 'If the police could find it, then it could give them some clues about the identity of the murderer.'

'I'm sure it would have been driven far out of London and abandoned somewhere,' said Aunt Lydia. 'Pushed into water, maybe, or even set on fire? They would have taken the drugs out and sold them before they did that, of course.' She sighed. 'These people are very good at escaping detection.'

'I keep thinking I'm missing something,' said Augusta.

'Such as what?'

'I don't know. That's the problem. Do you mind if I look in Sir Graywood's study?'

'What for?'

'A clue of some sort. Any clue.'

'Of course. I'll come with you.'

Augusta didn't want Aunt Lydia to accompany her. She didn't want to be watched as she searched through Sir Graywood's things.

Aunt Lydia led her to the study and flicked the light switch. Augusta glanced at the cricketing memorabilia on the walls and then made her way to the desk.

'Do you mind if I look through the drawers?' she asked.

'No, of course, Augusta. What are you looking for?'

'I really don't know. But I feel like I'll know when I see it. It may sound odd, but it's happened before.'

'Well, if you know what you're doing, then that's fine,' said Aunt Lydia. 'But I don't know what you'll actually find here.'

The desk drawers were all unlocked, and they held items of little interest. Pens, notebooks, a ball of string, a broken pair of spectacles, snuffboxes, a comb, some bullets, a cricketing almanac from 1919, a box of cigars and a tin of boiled sweets. Augusta took her time and Aunt Lydia lost interest and made herself comfortable in one of the leather chairs.

'It's not an easy room to spend much time in,' she said. 'In fact, I think this is the longest amount of time I've spent in here since Frederick's death.'

Augusta found a bunch of keys. Were they household keys or for something else? She slowly clasped her left hand around them as Aunt Lydia talked.

'It's just as Frederick left it,' said her aunt. 'I'd like to change it because it's a gentleman's room and not comfortable for a lady at all. But it was his room and changing it would somehow feel like an insult to him. Even though he's not here anymore.'

The keys were now clasped tightly in Augusta's hand. She continued looking in the drawer as if she hadn't yet found anything. Then, with a deft movement, she stood up and slipped her left hand into her pocket.

Then a photograph in a cabinet caught her eye. She stepped over to it. 'Those look like police officers,' she said.

'Oh yes. That's when Frederick's team played a police team. I don't know which one. It was before the war.'

'They played in their uniforms?'

'I don't think so. They must have changed into them after the match for the photograph.'

'It's just given me a thought,' said Augusta. She took her hand from her pocket, forgetting about the keys now. 'The most obvious culprit from that night. Why didn't I think of it before?'

'Who?'

'Constable Buller! The man who found your husband. He's the murderer!'

'A police officer?'

'A corrupt police officer! He knew Sir Graywood would be there that night. He must have been working for a gang to steal the cocaine. Goodness.'

'Augusta.' Her aunt beamed. 'You're so clever!'

'I don't know yet. We'll have to prove it. Please can I use this telephone?' She pointed to the telephone on the desk. 'I need to telephone my friend, Mr Fisher.'

'At this hour?'

'He'll still be awake.'

Augusta picked up the receiver and spoke to the operator.

Chapter 47

'I'M NOT SURE ABOUT CONSTABLE BULLER,' SAID Detective Inspector Jenkins at Scotland Yard the following morning.

'Why not?' asked Philip.

'I don't think he's the murdering type. He's clearly the corrupt type. But so are the other officers who Graywood paid off. Constables Milton, Edwards, Marshall, Harrison, Pugh and Ellman. Sergeant Finch—'

'Sergeant Finch was paid off, too?' asked Augusta. 'But he was the one investigating the case!'

'He was. It's a farce, isn't it? Sir Graywood paid him to ignore his nocturnal visits to the dockyard. Sergeant Wittman was paid off too.'

'Nine police officers,' said Philip. 'Many people knew about Sir Graywood's smuggling, didn't they? His son and second in command were in on it too, and I'm sure there must be more.'

'It seems it was an open secret,' said Augusta. 'And yet we took our time uncovering it.'

'Because there was a cover-up,' said Jenkins. 'If

everyone you speak to is lying, then it can take a while to get to the truth.'

'But will you interview Buller?' said Augusta. 'I agree he seems mild-mannered but you never know.'

'I agree,' said Philip. 'And if he accepted money from Sir Graywood, perhaps he accepted money from another smuggler, too. A rival one who wanted to get his hands on that shipment of cocaine.'

'We'll bring him in,' said Jenkins. 'And I'll let you know how we get on.' He cleared his throat. 'There's something I'd like to say to you, Mrs Peel.'

'Is there?'

'Yes. I would like to thank you. You found evidence that your uncle was smuggling cocaine, and you elicited a confession from Constable Buller which revealed a web of corruption in the Port of London Authority police force.'

'That's alright. I didn't elicit it, he just came into my shop and spoke.'

'But he chose you for a reason, Mrs Peel. You're approachable and that helped a great deal.'

She wanted to tell him he could be approachable too if he removed his permanent scowl, but she decided not to.

'If Buller is the murderer,' said Philip. 'Then could he have murdered Nancy Claydene?'

'I think so,' said Augusta. 'The two murders are similar. Both victims were struck on the back of the head with a heavy object.'

'News travels fast,' said Jenkins. 'I had no idea the details of Miss Claydene's murder were public knowledge yet.'

'But you agree the murders are the same?' Augusta asked him.

'Oh yes. Very similar indeed.'

'Miss Claydene was having an affair with Sir Graywood,' said Augusta. 'Perhaps he involved her with his smuggling operation.'

'It wouldn't surprise me if he did,' said Philip.

'If Buller was working for a rival smuggler, then perhaps he wanted her dead, too?' suggested Augusta. 'He could have ordered Buller to kill her.'

'Well, I'll see what Buller says about it all,' said Jenkins.

Augusta and Philip left Scotland Yard and walked along the riverside. Fluffy grey clouds in the blue sky threatened rain.

'I'd like to interview Buller myself,' said Philip. 'But as I'm no longer at Scotland Yard, then I just have to let them get on with it.'

'Remember how busy it kept you,' said Augusta.

'That's true. It put an end to my marriage, didn't it?'

They exchanged a glance and Augusta blushed. She felt awkward with Philip after their kiss the previous evening. She wondered if she should say something or pretend it hadn't happened.

Did he regret it?

'I forgot to explain more about those poison pen letters sent to Dr Lennox,' said Philip.

'Oh, there's no need to,' said Augusta. She looked out across the river to the grand white facade of the newly built London County Hall. 'They've nearly finished it,' she said, pointing to it.

'Looks good, doesn't it? Don't change the subject, Augusta. I want to discuss Dr Lennox.'

'I thought we'd forgotten about him?' She turned to him and smiled. Philip grinned. 'It would be nice to, wouldn't it? But I want to give you my explanation. It explains why I got so... oh, I don't know... frustrated, I suppose. And a little worried too. Over the past couple of weeks, I've spoken to a lot of people about him and I'm afraid to report he's quite a womaniser.'

'Oh.' Augusta felt disappointed that he'd charmed her.

'I'm afraid so. He promised marriage to a lady but went back on it, he had an affair with a clergyman's wife, and he had an illegitimate child with a colonel's daughter.'

'Oh dear.'

'I think the colonel could be the source of the poison pen letters, but I'm reluctant to identify the culprit because I think Dr Lennox deserves what he gets.'

'Even though he's a war hero?'

'As you said last night, Augusta. No one is perfect.'

Chapter 48

When Philip and Augusta returned to the shop, they found Dr Lennox chatting with Fred.

'Ah ha!' said Dr Lennox, spreading his arms wide. 'Just the people I came to see!'

The gesture irritated Augusta. 'Just the people for what?' she asked.

'The people I came to see. I have another letter for you, Mr Fisher, and I just wanted to ask you, Augusta, which restaurant you would like to dine at next Tuesday.'

She felt her stomach sink. 'Oh yes, I forgot I already have plans on Tuesday.'

She went over to the counter, took out Sparky's bag of birdseed and began feeding him.

Dr Lennox chuckled. 'He likes that, doesn't he? Erm... Wednesday?'

'I can't do Wednesday, I'm afraid.'

'Thursday?'

Augusta sighed and looked him in the eye. 'I'm sorry, Dr Lennox, but I think I'm going to be busy for quite a while.'

An awkward pause followed. Fred glanced up at the ceiling and Philip looked at the floor and scratched the back of his neck.

'Right,' said Dr Lennox eventually. 'That's absolutely fine, Augusta. There's no hurry at all. Take all the time you need to, er… be busy. And if you do fancy dinner some-time, then just let me know.'

She felt a pang of guilt. Then she remembered the broken promise of marriage, the clergyman's wife, and the illegitimate child.

'It was nice to see you again, Dr Lennox. Have a good day.'

'Absolutely. Goodbye Augusta.' He turned on his heel and everything fell quiet as he left the shop.

'Oh dear,' said Fred, once the door had closed again. 'Poor man.'

'I wouldn't feel sorry for him,' said Philip. 'And he forgot to give me his letter. Never mind. They all say the same thing, anyway.'

'I suppose I should visit Aunt Lydia,' said Augusta. 'I need to see how she's doing today. With Nancy Claydene gone and Rupert in custody, she doesn't really have anyone to talk to other than her staff.'

'Good idea,' said Philip.

'And for some reason, I took a bunch of keys from Sir Graywood's desk drawer last night.'

'Why?'

'I don't know. I think it's because I feel the urge to have a good look around that house. And if there are locked cupboards, I can open them. But it's difficult when Aunt Lydia is always there.'

'Why do you want to look around it?' asked Fred.

'Because, to my knowledge, it's never been searched by

the police. We all considered Sir Graywood's office to be the most important place, but there may be more clues in the house.'

'If Jenkins gets a confession from Buller, there may be no need,' said Philip. 'But good luck with it all the same.'

Chapter 49

THE CHAUFFEUR WAS POLISHING THE NAPIER LIMOUSINE again when Augusta arrived at her aunt's house.

'It's shiny enough to use as a shaving mirror,' said Augusta.

He pointed to the London Plane tree nearby. 'This isn't much good for it. Especially not this time of year when the leaves are falling. And the pigeons do their business on it too.'

'Has the stable in the mews not been converted into a garage yet?'

He shrugged. 'No space for it at the moment.'

Inside the house, Aunt Lydia was pleased to see her. 'Thank you for calling on me, Augusta. I appreciate it very much.' They sat in the burgundy and gold drawing room and the lean black cat stretched out on the hearthrug. 'I received a telegram from your father this morning.'

'Really?'

'Yes, I told him about Nancy's death and he sent his sympathies. It's only brief but thoughtful all the same. We should visit him.'

'We? You and I?'

'Yes. Having lost two people close to me, I'm realising how important family is. What happened between you was twenty years ago, Augusta. A lot has happened since then. And I think we've all changed, too.'

Augusta had accustomed herself to the idea she wouldn't see her family again. 'I would have to think about it,' she said. 'For quite a long time.'

'Of course, Augusta. But do give it some thought because you never know what can happen in life. It's awful living with regrets.' She sipped her tea and sighed. 'I really struggle to know what to think about Frederick. Obviously, I loved him very much, and his death was an unspeakable tragedy. But to discover he was caught up in all sorts of unpleasantness was quite devastating. I have to come to terms with the fact he wasn't a very good person. And that's difficult to accept.'

Once again, Augusta thought of his affair with Nancy Claydene. She felt keen to tell her aunt about it one day.

'We were married for fifteen years and I thought I knew him. But I didn't, did I? Desperately sad.'

Augusta stayed and drank tea with her a little while longer. Then, as it neared lunchtime, she prepared herself to leave.

'I'll visit you again soon, Aunt Lydia,' she said.

'Thank you, Augusta. You're a dear.'

After leaving the house, Augusta walked halfway along the street until she reached a narrow turning which led to the mews behind the grand Mayfair townhouses. In the eighteenth and nineteenth centuries, the mews had provided stables for carriages and horses as well as accommodation for the grooms and stable boys. But the arrival of the motor car had rendered them obsolete. Some had been converted to garages for cars, while others were now being used for storage.

Augusta walked along the cobbled alleyway and looked at the numbers on the old stable houses. Each had a number which corresponded to the number of the townhouse.

She reached number five. It was two storeys high and had scruffy, panelled wooden doors which were padlocked. Beyond it, Augusta could see the upper two storeys of Aunt Lydia's house.

'I'm sorry Aunt Lydia,' she whispered as she pulled the bunch of keys from her bag. 'But I don't trust you.'

It took a while to find the right key for the rusty padlock. Just as Augusta was doubting she had the key, the padlock opened.

She pulled open one of the wooden doors and its hinges creaked.

The chauffeur hadn't lied to her, there was no space in there for Aunt Lydia's car.

As Augusta pulled the door open further, daylight fell on the twin round headlamps of a shabby Ford Model T van.

Chapter 50

Was it the same van Sir Graywood had driven to West India Dock on that fateful evening? Augusta wished now she'd asked Constable Buller for a description of it.

The van in front of her was bottle green. The paintwork was grimy and rusting in places. Augusta stepped into the garage and closed the door behind her. The smell of oil was strong and dusty cobwebs hung from the ceiling.

She took a torch from her handbag and examined the van. Lettering on its side had been painted over, but the ridged edging of the letters remained. It had once said, "Lawson and Co, Grocers."

There was nothing to suggest this had been the van which Sir Graywood had used on the night of his death. Augusta could only be certain if the cases of cocaine were still inside.

There wasn't much space to move around the van. Augusta walked to the rear and was dismayed to discover there was no room to open the doors at the back. The van was parked too closely against the wall.

Augusta shone her torch at the front of the van and

saw a three-foot gap between the radiator and the door. She had experience of driving Fords in the war and knew what to do. She stepped over to the driver's door, opened it, then squeezed and pushed the lever which rose out of the floor by the driver's seat. By moving the lever, she was releasing the parking brake and would be able to move the vehicle forward so she could access the doors at the back.

Augusta went to the back of the van and rested her handbag and torch on the floor. She squeezed in between the van and the wall with her back against the van and her hands on the wall. Then she pushed backwards.

Nothing happened.

She tried again, pushing and straining with all her might. But the van was too heavy.

Augusta grew frustrated. She tried a jolting motion, using short, sharp shoves with her body to budge the van.

Eventually, there was movement. She braced herself with her hands on the wall and pushed until she felt the veins at the front of her head would burst. The van rolled a little more.

Surely there was space to open a door now.

Dizzy from the exertion, Augusta leant against the wall to recover. Then she picked up her torch and turned a handle on the back of the van. There wasn't enough space to fully open the door, but there was enough space to open the door wide enough and peer in.

The torch's beam fell on the wooden side of a tea chest. Its lid had been prised open and not properly replaced.

Augusta wedged herself through the gap in the door and managed to get closer to the tea chest. She pushed the lid out of the way. She couldn't get close enough to see into the chest, but she could get her hand inside.

Cautiously, she pushed her hand down into the tea

chest. Her fingers met with sawdust. She pushed her way in further and got her hand in lower, moving it around in the hope she could get to something other than sawdust.

And then her fingers caught on something smooth.

She clasped her hand around it and pulled it out.

It was a little glass bottle with a German label on it: "Beruhigende Medizin".

She heard the hinges of the door creak and daylight flooded into the garage.

Augusta caught her breath. She'd been discovered.

Chapter 51

AUGUSTA STEPPED OUT FROM BEHIND THE VAN TO SEE A figure in an overcoat silhouetted in the doorway.

It was Aunt Lydia.

'Augusta?' she said. 'What are you doing in here?'

'I found the van,' she said. 'The van which Sir Graywood drove that night.'

Aunt Lydia stepped into the garage and stared at the vehicle, as if she hadn't seen it before.

'How did it get here?'

'His murderer hid it here,' said Augusta. 'We need to tell the police.'

'No, we don't.' Aunt Lydia's voice changed to a low, quiet tone. She pulled something from her pocket. Light glinted on metal in her hand. Augusta's stomach knotted as she realised it was a pistol.

She took in a breath and slowed her pounding heart. 'If you fire that, everyone around us will hear,' she said. 'It will echo in this garage and reverberate around the mews and the houses and someone will come running immediately.'

Aunt Lydia pointed the pistol at her. Her face fixed in an impassive stare.

Augusta avoided looking at the gun and concentrated on making her aunt talk. 'You've been very clever, Aunt Lydia. I'm really impressed.'

It took a moment for the mask to crack. 'Impressed?'

'Yes. You've outwitted the dockyard police and Scotland Yard. No one ever suspected you.'

'But you did.'

'Tell me why you did it.'

Aunt Lydia sighed. 'You're fortunate you never knew Frederick, Augusta. He was an abominable man. The affairs... the smuggling...'

'You knew about all that?'

'Of course I knew about it all. I'm not stupid. The smuggling has gone on for a while, as you've probably guessed. He told me he needed to do it because the company was struggling for money. It almost went bankrupt during the war and never really regained the success it'd had before. So I knew about it, but I didn't get involved. I left him to get on with whatever he needed to. And I mistakenly believed he'd turned his fortunes around. So when I discovered there was no money after his death.... well that came as a shock.'

'You were hoping you would benefit from the wealth he left?'

'Of course! I deserved it, Augusta. I'd put up with him for a long, long time. So it was a bitter blow when I discovered there was nothing.'

Augusta reasoned that the longer she kept Aunt Lydia talking, the less likely she was to fire the pistol. She felt encouraged, but her heart still pounded and her mouth felt dry. 'When did you find out about the affair with Nancy?' she asked.

'A few months ago. I knew Frederick had been unfaithful in the past, but when it's with someone you thought was a friend... well, that's very different. I couldn't bear Nancy visiting and pretending to be my friend when all along she was having an affair with my husband. The deceit angered me so much that I wanted to punish them for it. I confronted Frederick, but he denied it all. He told me I was imagining things, and I was growing hysterical in my old age. Oh, the things he said, Augusta! He could be vile.

'It was the belittling which angered me the most. I couldn't bear it. It was a miserable existence, and I wanted to get out of it. I'd considered murdering him for a while.'

'Really?'

'Yes, I know it sounds a little extreme to someone mild mannered like you, Augusta. But I'm afraid it's the sort of person I am. I'm like a coiled spring. I can only be wound up so much before I simply just... snap.'

'So you planned his murder extremely well. It fooled everyone.'

'Oh yes, I'm good at planning things.'

'How did you do it?'

'I knew that whenever he planned to stay overnight at his club, it was when he was collecting a shipment. So that night, I decided to join him.'

Chapter 52

'I KNEW FREDERICK KEPT THE VAN IN AN OLD WAREHOUSE in Limehouse,' said Aunt Lydia. 'So I got a taxi there late that night and waited for him in the van. I just sat there in the passenger seat until he turned up. He was rather surprised to see me!'

'Did he ask you to leave?' asked Augusta.

'Oh yes. He told me it was dangerous and told me to go home. I refused. He didn't have time to argue with me because he'd agreed times with the nightwatchmen at the dock. They had to let him in at a certain time and stay out of the way, you see. So he had to take me with him. I'd hidden the cricket bat in the cabin behind the seats.'

'Cricket bat?'

'Yes. That's what I hit him with. He would have seen it there if he'd deliberately looked for it. But it was dark, and he was in a hurry, so he didn't notice it. When we approached the gates to the dockyard, he told me to duck down in my seat so the nightwatchman wouldn't see me. He didn't want to risk me getting into trouble as well as him. It was a very risky business. There was always the danger someone would be tipped off and he'd be discovered.

'We drove up to the ship and he told me to wait in the van while he went on board and carried out the tea chests. It didn't take long, about twenty minutes, I suppose. Then, when he was all done, I got out of the van and hid the cricket bat beneath my overcoat. It was very dark, neither of us could see much. But he had a torch with him.

'He told me to get back in the van because it was time to leave. As he turned to get into the driver's side, I just wielded the bat.'

Augusta winced.

'I couldn't really see what I was doing, but I just continued lashing out. He fell to the floor quickly. It had taken him by surprise.'

The coolness of Aunt Lydia's manner chilled Augusta. Her tears before now had clearly been an act.

'I threw the cricket bat into the water,' continued Aunt Lydia. 'Then I got into the van and drove off. The dockyard gates had been left unlocked for Frederick, so it was easy. You're probably surprised I can drive, Augusta. But I learned during the war, as you did too, I expect. We all had to learn these skills and put ourselves to good use while the men were away, didn't we? Anyway, I hadn't really thought about what to do with the van. Quite unlike me, really. I had only thought about the murder.

'I drove home, and the Napier was in here. So I had to drive it out and bring the van in. Then I took the Napier around to the front of the house. I'm quite astonished nobody came out to see what was going on. But everybody was sound asleep, and you know what London's like, Augusta, everyone minds their own business.'

'How did you explain it to the chauffeur?' said

Augusta. 'He must have wondered why the car was parked out the front.'

'I told him I was using the garage for storage and he was to keep out of there. I wish now I had abandoned the van somewhere or set it on fire, but I hadn't really thought the plan through. And I wanted to get rid of the cocaine, but I had no idea who to sell it to. And it would have looked suspicious. I knew I would have to get rid of the van and the drugs eventually, but I made the mistake of delaying it. And now you've found it Augusta.'

Her hand with the pistol in it had dropped a little while she'd been talking. But now she raised it again.

'And Nancy Claydene?' asked Augusta.

Aunt Lydia groaned. 'I couldn't bear the way she kept visiting me after Frederick's death! She sat there in my drawing room, eating my grapes and pretending to be upset for me. And I knew that all along she was just upset about him. She was a deceitful woman. She cared nothing for me or my feelings.'

'Couldn't you have just broken up the friendship?'

'Yes. But it wouldn't have been enough. She deserved to be punished! She visited me the day before her death and let slip that she would be at the shop on her own. She was complaining about it as usual. She didn't like having to do any work. So yesterday, shortly before closing time, I took a taxi to her shop. I concealed a cricket bat beneath my overcoat.'

'Another cricket bat?'

'Yes. Frederick had plenty of them. It was almost the end of the day, and Nancy was getting ready to close the shop. She was surprised to see me there, but I told her I was looking for a new hat. When she turned away, I hit her with the bat. It was very risky, of course. Someone could have seen. But I was angry. It's difficult to think straight when you're angry. I dragged her into the little room at the back and found a little door there which led out into an alleyway. So that's the way I went. I shoved the bat in a dustbin. It's probably still there.'

Augusta felt stunned. 'Goodness,' she said. 'And Uncle Noel?'

'Uncle Noel?'

'Yes. I always wondered what happened to him.'

'He fell out of a rowing boat on Lake Ullswater.'

'Were you with him at the time?'

'Yes.'

'How did it happen?'

'I asked to change ends. So he stood up, but I remained sitting. I stuck my leg out, and he lost his balance. He couldn't swim.'

'You knocked him in?'

'Your Uncle Noel was a drinker, Augusta. A terrible man. He wouldn't have known anything. He sank like a stone.'

Augusta felt nauseous.

'Anyway. Now I've told you everything, Augusta. I shall have to get rid of you, too. No one can find you and the van here. You're going to drive it somewhere.'

Augusta had hoped someone would arrive at the garage while she and Aunt Lydia were talking. Philip knew she was here, but would have no idea about the predicament she was in.

No one was coming to rescue her.

'Alright then.' She didn't want to protest while a gun was pointed at her. 'Where shall we go, Aunt Lydia?'

She climbed into the driver's seat and Aunt Lydia cranked the engine. To Augusta's disappointment, it stuttered into life.

Aunt Lydia climbed into the passenger seat next to her and held the gun in her lap.

'Oops,' said Augusta over the noise of the engine. 'My handbag!'

'You don't need it! Just drive!'

'But if someone finds it, then it's evidence I've been here, isn't it? They'll ask you questions.'

'Fine. But be quick.'

Augusta got out of the van and fetched her handbag from the back of the garage. While she was stooped down, she pulled a spare hatpin from her handbag. Holding her breath from the cloud of exhaust fumes, she jabbed the hatpin with all her might into the rear tyre. After three quick jabs, the hatpin was bent.

'Hurry up!'

Augusta heard panic in Aunt Lydia's voice. She wanted her aunt to remain calm while she had a gun in her hand.

'Here I am,' said Augusta, climbing back into the van. 'Let's go.'

Chapter 53

AUGUSTA STEERED THE VAN OUT OF THE GARAGE AND INTO the narrow, cobbled road in the mews.

'We need to get out to the countryside,' shouted Aunt Lydia over the engine. 'Head for Richmond Park.'

'Richmond Park? Countryside?'

'It's large. And parts of it are remote.'

They turned into the main street and Augusta wondered when the tyre was going to deflate.

'Faster!' said Aunt Lydia.

'If I go too fast, I'll draw attention to us.'

'But you can go faster than this.'

They headed towards Grosvenor Square and the van felt fine. Augusta wondered if she had made a big enough hole in the tyre. Perhaps it was just a small hole and the tyre would take hours to deflate?

'Where are you going?' asked Aunt Lydia as they entered Grosvenor Square.

'I'm heading for Oxford Street and then I can turn west on there.'

'No, Piccadilly is quicker.'

'Is it?' Augusta felt happy to drive slowly and act stupid. She needed to dawdle. 'I'll need to go all the way around the square then.'

'No, you don't, you can just turn right here. Oh, too late! Now you have to go all the way around the square.'

They were halfway around it when Augusta felt resistance from the van. It was slowing and dragging to the right.

'Speed up Augusta!'

'I can't. There's something wrong. I think we have a flat tyre.'

'Oh, good grief. Just keep driving.'

'I can't!' A man with a barrow waved at them and pointed at the wheels. 'Look, he's telling us there's something wrong. We must have a flat tyre. When did you last inflate them?'

'Me? Inflate a tyre?'

'They need inflating regularly on these vans.'

Augusta pulled the van to a stop and got out. She had no intention of getting back in again.

To her satisfaction, she saw the rear tyre was completely deflated.

'It's flat!' she called out.

Aunt Lydia joined her. Her hands in her pockets. 'Then we need someone to replace it,' she said. 'Quickly!'

'Who?'

'I don't know. Someone must have a spare tyre around here.'

Augusta began to walk away. She followed the railings which ran around the little park in the centre of the square.

'Augusta!' called out her aunt.

'I'm getting help!' she called out.

She took in a deep breath, relieved to be away. But she somehow needed to disarm Aunt Lydia.

She saw a police box on the corner and ran towards it.

'Augusta!' Aunt Lydia was behind her.

'Help!' Augusta called out. 'Help! This lady has a gun!'

A constable stepped out. 'What is it, madam?'

Augusta turned to see Aunt Lydia pointing the pistol at both her and the constable. He blew his whistle. 'Drop the gun!' he shouted.

'No!'

'Officers are on their way! Drop it now!'

'I won't!'

A deafening shot ran out. The constable cursed, and Augusta ducked. She couldn't see where the shot had gone, but she and the constable were fine.

'I apologise for my language, madam. But I think we're dealing with a madwoman.'

The man with the barrow was behind Aunt Lydia. He abandoned the barrow and ran towards her. Augusta wanted to warn him to be careful, but she didn't want to alert her aunt to his presence.

'You betrayed me, Augusta!' cried out Aunt Lydia. 'I should have known better than to trust you! You abandoned your family once and now you've done it again!'

Another shot rang out.

Augusta and the constable dropped to the ground. Augusta looked up to see the man behind Aunt Lydia tackle her to the ground.

She toppled over with a cry. In an instant, the constable jumped to his feet and ran over to her.

'She's disarmed!' he shouted as he snatched the pistol from her.

Augusta remained on the ground. She exhaled with

relief and rested her head on her hands as tears sprung into her eyes.

Chapter 54

'IT MUST HAVE BEEN DIFFICULT TO SUSPECT YOUR OWN AUNT of murder, Augusta,' said Philip. 'Why did you even consider her?'

She sat with Philip in his office with Fred. She'd just returned from Scotland Yard to explain her role in the afternoon's events. Now, it was early evening and long golden sunbeams shone on the wall above Philip's desk.

'I first grew suspicious when I was in Sir Graywood's study,' said Augusta. 'I noticed a blue and white porcelain plate on the wall and it looked out of place.'

'How?'

'It was hanging alongside some autographed cricket bats. I felt sure Sir Graywood wouldn't have put it there. And it occurred to me that someone could have hung the plate there to cover a gap. If one of the cricket bats had been removed, then there would have been spare nails or holes in the wall. An obvious gap.'

'So your aunt took down the cricket bat and put something there in its place in the hope no one would notice?' said Philip.

'Yes,' said Augusta. 'And that made me realise a cricket bat was missing. It occurred to me it would make a good murder weapon, and I knew Sir Graywood had been killed with a heavy blunt object. But I didn't think of this detail, at the time. It was only when the second cricket bat disappeared after Nancy Claydene's murder that my mind worked on it some more.'

'There was another plate in its place?'

'No, not this time. Just a gap and the nails were still in the wall. Perhaps Aunt Lydia hadn't got round to putting a plate there yet. I noticed this when I requested to look around Sir Graywood's study last night. Aunt Lydia didn't like me doing it, of course, and that's why she accompanied me. In fact, I think she was quite wary of me by that point. So I came up with Constable Buller as the culprit to distract her.'

'Remarkable!' said Philip with a grin. 'So she overheard you telephone me from Graywood's study, and she was therefore convinced you thought Buller was the killer.'

'Yes,' said Augusta. 'I think she trusted me again after that.'

'But you didn't trust her.'

'No. And when she told me about Nancy Claydene's death, she knew quite a bit of detail about the cause of her death and where the body was found. When I mentioned some of this to Detective Inspector Jenkins, he remarked he was surprised it was public knowledge.'

'She knew the details because she'd been there,' said Fred.

'Exactly. And who even told her about Miss Claydene's murder?'

'That's a good point,' said Philip. 'What time did she telephone you, Augusta, about half-past nine?'

'That's right.' Augusta blushed a little, recalling Philip had been there at the time.

'And the body of Miss Claydene was discovered some time after her shop was supposed to have closed,' said Philip. 'About seven? Her cause of death wouldn't have been confirmed until a doctor had properly examined the body. It's suspicious that Lady Graywood knew a lot of detail quite quickly.'

'And I suspected Aunt Lydia knew about her husband's smuggling activities,' said Augusta. 'Everyone else around him seemed to know. And I reasoned that if she knew about his affair with Nancy, then she had a motive for killing both her husband and Miss Claydene. The death of her first husband was suspicious, too. Once I suspected she'd murdered her husband and friend, I wondered if she'd had something to do with Uncle Noel's death as well.'

'And it turned out she did,' said Philip.

Harriet brought in a tray of tea.

'Marvellous, thank you Harriet,' said Fred. 'You make the best tea.'

'And of course the most obvious clue was the van,' said Philip. 'I expect Lady Graywood is very annoyed she didn't get rid of it.'

'The van caused a problem for her,' said Augusta. 'She didn't know what to do with it. I kept thinking about the van. The police never found it abandoned. So I wondered if the murderer had hidden it. And then I thought about where. I'd noticed Lady Graywood's chauffeur wasn't happy with her car being kept on the street beneath a tree. He was always cleaning and polishing it. So I asked him why it wasn't kept in the garage. When he told me there was no space for the car, I wanted to find out what was being stored there.'

'The van,' said Philip. 'And it makes perfect sense. Lady Graywood's home was never searched by the police. She'd hoped they wouldn't suspect her, and they never did.'

'Hello?' came a lady's voice from the shop downstairs.

'I thought you locked up, Fred,' said Augusta.

'Oh, I'm sorry, I thought you did, Augusta! I'll go down.'

'No, it's alright. I'll go. I think I recognise the voice.'

Augusta went downstairs to the shop to find Lady Hereford there in her bath chair with her nurse by her side. 'Augusta! I've just got a copy of the evening paper.' She brandished it at her. 'It says that Lady Graywood was arrested in Grosvenor Square this afternoon with a gun! And apparently she's been arrested for her husband's murder and the murder of Miss Claydene! Did you know about this?'

'Yes,' said Augusta. 'I've just returned from Scotland Yard where we discussed it all.'

'Did you have a part to play in it?'

'A little. I can tell you all about it, we're just upstairs celebrating.'

'Upstairs? I can't get upstairs. Tell them to come down here so I can join in.'

A short while later, everyone gathered in the shop.

'I don't know why we're drinking tea,' said Lady Hereford. 'It should be champagne.'

'It's very nice tea,' said Philip.

'Yes, it is,' said Lady Hereford. 'Some of the nicest I've ever drunk, actually.'

'Harriet made it,' said Fred.

'Well done, Harriet!' said Lady Hereford. 'But celebrations like this call for something stronger.'

'I'll go out and buy a bottle,' said Philip.

'Get two,' said Lady Hereford.

A short while later, the two bottles of champagne had been drunk. Lady Hereford returned to her suite at the Russell Hotel, and Fred and Harriet went to the cinema.

Augusta picked up Sparky's cage from the counter. 'What a long day,' she said.

'I'm very proud of you, Augusta,' said Philip.

'Thank you.'

He stepped closer and kissed her. She felt happy he wanted to kiss her again. His embrace felt warm and comforting.

'I couldn't have done it without you,' she said.

'Yes, you could have.' They walked across the shop towards the door.

'I disagree.'

'Do you? Well, perhaps we could continue our disagreement over dinner tonight. What do you say?'

She stopped by the door. 'I'd love to, Philip.'

'Good. And if I have an annoying laugh, you'll tell me, won't you? Don't drop me like a stone like you did with poor old Dr Lennox.'

Augusta grinned and took his hand. 'I could never do that, Philip.'

The End

~

229

Historical Note

London's docks have been a vital part of the city's history for nearly two thousand years.

London's role as a port began in Roman times when small ships docked at quays along the Thames. By the late nineteenth century, the docks stretched an impressive twenty-six miles from central London to Tilbury, making it one of the busiest ports in the world.

Geoffrey Chaucer, best known for writing *The Canterbury Tales*, was appointed controller of customs for the Port of London in 1374, overseeing the goods moving in and out of the city. He held the post for twelve years.

The first purpose-built dock was built in Rotherhithe during the seventeenth century. London's docks continued to expand after this, with the West India Docks opening in the early nineteenth century to handle goods from the British West Indies (a group of Caribbean islands colonised by the British). In later years, West India Docks handled ships from all over the world. At their peak, London's docks employed around 100,000 people. Generations of families in east and south London worked at the docks.

By the 1960s, containerisation and the decline of Britain's manufacturing industries made the docks obsolete. Ships grew too large to navigate the Thames, and the once-thriving dockyards fell silent. The area underwent a dramatic transformation in the 1980s, with the creation of Canary Wharf as a business district and London City Airport at the Royal Docks. Today, many old docks have been repurposed into housing, offices, and attractions like the Museum of London Docklands. Yet the Port of Tilbury remains operational, ranking as the UK's third-largest port.

London's docks had their own police force. The first dock police were established in 1802 at the West India Docks, and by 1909, the various forces merged to become the Port of London Authority police, employing a thousand officers at their peak. As the docks declined, so did the force, which was eventually downsized and renamed the Port of Tilbury Police in 1992.

The statue of Achilles in Hyde Park is a larger-than-life sculpture which was unveiled in 1822. It caused quite a stir as London's first nude statue in modern times. The statue celebrated the Duke of Wellington's military victories, but Achilles caused some scandal at the time as all he wore was a fig leaf!

Mayfair takes its name from the annual May fair, held there during the seventeenth and eighteenth centuries. The Grosvenor family acquired the land and, in the eighteenth century, transformed it into a prestigious residential district for the upper classes. Grosvenor Square, with its grand townhouses, became one of London's most fashionable addresses until the Second World War. After the war, many of these luxurious homes found new life as embassies and commercial properties.

From 1938 to 2017, Grosvenor Square housed the United States Embassy. The embassy is now located in a new building in Battersea, south of the river. During the Second World War, General Dwight D. Eisenhower established a military headquarters in Grosvenor Square, which remained active until 2009. The square also features statues of American presidents Eisenhower, Franklin D. Roosevelt, and Ronald Reagan, reflecting its long association with Anglo-American relations.

Thank you

Thank you for reading this Augusta Peel mystery, I really hope you enjoyed it!

Would you like to know when I release new books? Here are some ways to stay updated:

- Like my Facebook page: facebook.com/ emilyorganwriter
- Follow me on Goodreads: goodreads.com/emily_organ
- Follow me on BookBub: bookbub.com/authors/emily-organ
- View my other books here: emilyorgan.com

And if you have a moment, I would be very grateful if you would leave a quick review online. Honest reviews of my books help other readers discover them too!

Coming soon!

The Whitechapel Widow
An Emma Langley Victorian Mystery Book 1

From the bestselling author of Penny Green comes a spellbinding new Victorian mystery series introducing Emma Langley.

London hunts the Ripper. A widow hunts her husband's killer.

London, 1888. While Jack the Ripper's reign of terror grips the city, Emma Langley's world shatters when her husband is found murdered in Whitechapel. But grief is quickly overshadowed by a startling discovery: William Langley was not the man she thought she knew.

As panic fills London's streets, Emma delves into her husband's secret life, uncovering a web of lies that stretches from glittering society drawing rooms to the seedy gambling dens of the East End. Aided by Penny Green, a former reporter with a nose for trouble, Emma follows a trail of blackmail and corruption.

But exposing her husband's killer could make her the next victim and in the shadows of gaslit streets, a murderer waits, ready to strike again…

Find out more here: mybook.to/whitechapel-widow

Also by Emily Organ

Penny Green Series:

Limelight
The Rookery
The Maid's Secret
The Inventor
Curse of the Poppy
The Bermondsey Poisoner
An Unwelcome Guest
Death at the Workhouse
The Gang of St Bride's
Murder in Ratcliffe
The Egyptian Mystery
The Camden Spiritualist

Penny Green and Emma Langley Series:

The Whitechapel Widow

Churchill & Pemberley Series:

Also by Emily Organ

Tragedy at Piddleton Hotel
Murder in Cold Mud
Puzzle in Poppleford Wood
Trouble in the Churchyard
Wheels of Peril
The Poisoned Peer
Fiasco at the Jam Factory
Disaster at the Christmas Dinner
Christmas Calamity at the Vicarage (novella)

Writing as Martha Bond

Lottie Sprigg Travels Mystery Series:

Murder in Venice
Murder in Paris
Murder in Cairo
Murder in Monaco
Murder in Vienna

Lottie Sprigg Country House Mystery Series:

Murder in the Library
Murder in the Grotto
Murder in the Maze
Murder in the Bay

Printed in Great Britain
by Amazon

53047488R00139